TAMING

TO TAME A SHIFTER
BOOK 1

Taming

A.K. KOONCE

To Elana

AK Koonce

Taming

Copyright 2018 A.K. Koonce

All Rights Reserved

Cover design by Killer Book Covers

Editing by Varankor Editing & Editing & Ms. Correct All's Editing and Proofreading Services

No portion of this book may be reproduced in any form without express written permission from the author. Any unauthorized use of this material is prohibited.

This is a work of fiction. Names, characters, places, and incidents either are the products of the author's imagination or are used fictitiously. Any resemblance to actual persons, living or dead, businesses, companies, events or locales is entirely coincidental.

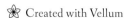 Created with Vellum

CONTENTS

1. Beautiful Monsters — 1
2. Sell-Those-Fucking-Dragons-So-Arlow-Can-Afford-To-Live Day — 11
3. The Transformation — 30
4. The Shifters and the Mage — 38
5. Ridiculous Men — 46
6. The Other Mage — 51
7. The Sweet One — 61
8. Reckless Emotions — 75
9. Ignoring Reality — 100
10. Between a Dream and Reality — 105
11. Her Honorable Word — 112
12. When Pasts Collide — 116
13. Faking It — 124
14. As White as Snow — 131
15. The Favorite — 143
16. The Mage — 154
17. His Filthy Mouth — 160
18. Flaws and Fuck Ups — 178
19. Personal Space — 185
20. Her Demons — 193

Author's Note — 203
Kreedence — 205
Also by A.K. Koonce — 209
About A.K. Koonce — 211

Dedicated to my mom. I bet she thought I'd outgrow that weird dragon phase.

ONE

BEAUTIFUL MONSTERS

White flashes of moonlight glint against the glossy surface of the large object in the old mage's palms. Interest fires all through my veins as she lowers it into the dirt, pushing at the dust until it makes a nice mound over the three items. She pats the dirt sweetly once more before turning away, her long dress skimming against the ground as she returns to the dark cottage. Her white hair sways against her back as she leaves, never once looking out at the road where I stand.

I'm a drifter. In a way, I've been a drifter my entire life. In the last five years, I've taken the job pretty seriously though. This small, quiet village within the Kingdom of Minden is nice, unnoticeable, and easy for someone who wants to disappear to do just that.

That's what I love about it.

This mage, Agatha, may be as old and dusty as this village itself, but she's my only friend. I came to check on her. Every few days I stop by to visit with her and gossip about who the Prince is sleeping with now and why it isn't me. *I'm wasting the beautiful curves of my youth* as she likes to tell me. I don't have the heart to tell the blind woman that the Prince isn't nearly as attractive as she thinks he is.

I might be a little bit of a bitch sometimes, but I'm not about to crush an old woman's fantasies. That's just cruel.

That's what I came here for: mindless chatter. Until Aggie started ominously burying something in her front yard. People only bury things for two reasons: to remember what they once had, or to hide what they once had.

The thin material of my dress brushes lightly against my thighs as I quietly make my way up the dirt path. A few overgrown bushes line the front yard, concealing one window and skimming against the glass of the other. Not that she could see me even if she looked out.

But she's a mage. A powerful mage. Much stronger than myself.

If she wanted to know what waited outside her little home, she would.

Hesitantly, I linger near the dirt that's piled over the object she buried. My gaze shifts to the arched front door. I came here for a visit with a friend.

I don't have many friends. Okay I don't have any aside from Aggie if I'm being honest. But fuck, she buried something under the light of the full moon. She all but did a ritual out here with a sacrificial goat. She could have disposed of them in a clandestine place, but she didn't. I can't just ignore that.

I lower myself, falling onto my hands and knees, and begin clawing at the dry dirt. It's a rapid and almost manic drive to find out what lies here. My conscience is quickly pushed aside as the dirt sinks into my nails with each handful of earth I rip away. The clinking sound of my bracelets makes my nerves skitter with every sound they make. A smooth curve beneath rocky particles of dirt glides against my fingertips. My palm sweeps over the hard surface once more, pushing aside the grit to see three objects underneath.

They're ... eggs.

Enormous eggs.

Large animals are worth a large price.

The animal trader in me is already mentally calculating what a beast this size could be worth. Imagine what three of them would be valued at.

With both hands, I try to steal away the top one, my arms aching as I realize the monstrous eggs are just as heavy as they look. My gaze flickers back to the golden glow of Agatha's front window. I could come back for the other two, but it's a mile-long walk. Would she come back out tonight?

I pull at the end of my skirt and quickly try to pile the three eggs into the thin material. A tearing sound rips through the silence, but as I stand, they hold in place against my body; straining against the cloth but not falling to the ground.

I'd hate to harm one of them.

I feel like an asshole. Who steals from a blind woman? Who does that?

... I do.

Why would Agatha bury them? She isn't as familiar with creatures as I am. Perhaps she thought they were useless. She's blind, so perhaps she didn't realize they were eggs at all.

But she's also a mage. So it's even more likely she knew what these things were and wanted to rid herself of them as quickly as possible.

I, on the other hand, am not about to throw away money, or the lives of whatever these animals may grow up to be.

Their lives will be worth living. I want to make a profit of course, but honestly, I just can't stand the thought of not helping them. I don't show it, but my little, slightly selfish heart loves these types of mysterious creatures.

Raising and selling magical animals is just a business for me. I can't get attached. I have to make a living in this world the only way I know how.

On awkward steps, and with aching arms, I carry the boulder like eggs home. The dark forest surrounds me, shutting out the majority of the moonlight and making me stumble more than once before my small shack comes into view.

Glowing embers of ruby eyes greet me as I get closer. The sweet little hellhound rubs his warm temple against my thigh as I pass, but I don't have a free arm to return the affection to my pet.

The dark and fuming hellhound, Grim, might just be the love of my life. It's a pathetic love life that I'm leading, I'll admit.

With the force of my hip, I bump open the door. A creaking cry comes from the hinges, and I don't bother closing it behind me as I settle in near the dwindling embers of the fire. The one room home is tiny with a cot on the far left side of the room and a worn and rickety kitchen table on the other side. The small fire easily warms the abandoned shack that I made my home.

The smooth curve of one of the eggs fills my hands. My own reflection peers at me on the iron like surface. The two others glisten near the fire. In the lighting, I can really make out their details. One's a pure white color. It shimmers like fresh snow while the one nestled next to it is as dark as blood. The third one, the one that I hold in my hands, is a consuming deep smoky tone.

They're shining and beautiful.

"But what are they?" I whisper to myself.

I have a thing for creatures, the dangerous and the unique, and I've never seen an egg this large. It's even bigger than an ostrich egg. Its structure seems thicker as well. I hold it close to my chest, and my eyes fall closed as a deep breath fills my lungs.

My magic is quiet within me. I've hidden it away and tried to save it up for when I know I'll really need it in the future.

It's there though. A numb sort of tingling feeling of power stings through my body.

A blur of a thousand images flickers through my mind. I search past them all until one faded image pulls to the front.

My sight shows me three colossal animals. Their wingspan is the size of the run-down shack that I've called home for the past year. Thick scales cover their bodies like proud armor. Long talons and sharp teeth lash down from the heavens, preparing to scoop up their next prey.

"Dragons." My eyes open once more, the depths of my blue irises are inky in the reflection of its glossy shell.

A strong and quick beat begins to take over my heart.

They're rare.

Deadly.

Expensive.

I've never sold a dragon before. The most I've ever gotten for a magical creature was a year's worth of income for a pegasus. Would have been more if it was a unicorn, but the buyer didn't believe me when I said its horn was just underdeveloped.

A dragon could pay for a new life, though. A real life. Imagine how I could live.

With three dragons, I could start over. No longer would I be a drifter running from her past. I could have a home. A family.

A *life*.

A smile pulls at my lips, and I've already made up my mind.

Without another thought, I toss the onyx egg into the fire.

Mages no longer have the darling little reputation that the generations before us had. No, we're feared. My mother hid me away to protect me, but it weakened my powers. When I was older, I studied magic and magical creatures. Studying magical creatures was the safest form of magic I could think of to continue to stay under the radar of those who hunt us. My actual powers grew stronger with the help of Kreedence. I thought he cared about me, but I know now that that was a lie.

My lip curls as I think of the man I thought I loved. I push the thoughts from my mind. It's an old chapter of my life and I grew from it. I learned more about my trade because of it.

I know creatures from all over the world. It's a specialty of mine.

And I know heat is needed for dragons to survive.

Maybe that's why Agatha disposed of them. Maybe she couldn't get them to hatch.

A cold summer breeze shakes against the worn, open door, threatening to tear it from its weak hinges as it drifts back and forth. The wind catches against my dark hair, but all my focus is on the flames caressing the inky shell.

Grit and dirt of the old floorboards shift against my fingertips as I move closer to the shining black egg.

Prayers like I've never said before stream through my

mind to whatever goddess my mother loved so much. I pray hard, wishing like hell the little creature will survive the heat and grow stronger from the kiss of the fire

The smallest of lines crack against the surface, making me gasp.

The heat stings my cheeks as I peer into the heart of the embers.

A breath is long forgotten in my lungs.

Without blinking, I stare hard with impatience.

Sharp nails pierce through the shell, thrusting through it until its whole leg is revealed and ripping off the imprisonment of its small home.

A quiet but powerful hum of a roar reverberates through the egg. Strong wings burst from its remaining surroundings and the tiny creature looks up at me with crystal-like eyes. Curiosity is in its gaze as it studies me for several seconds.

I shuffle quickly, reaching up on the table until I find the only food I have. I rip the meat into a thin shred, and with careful movements, I extend the offering to the little beast.

"Eat," I say in a quiet, gentle voice. It's a tone I'd never use with humans. As deadly as a dragon might be, humans are far worse creatures.

Yes, animals are much easier to speak with.

Bobble, the white tumid fish on my bedside table watches the beast with wide fearful eyes. His gaze is more bulging than normal if that's possible. The fat little fish looks like its puffy body is filled entirely with anxiety in this moment.

The dragon crawls out of the flames, shaking off the ash once it's on the floor next to me. A ticking sound announces its small steps as its talons hit the boards. Its head is the size of my palm, and its sharp teeth rake against my fingertips as it nibbles cautiously at the strip of dry meat in my hand.

Warm, golden firelight flashes across its eyes and I lean in even closer to the creature. One eye is a pale blue and one is a warm honey color. It's unique and beautiful. I've seen the iris mutation in dogs, but it isn't common. It keeps its gaze locked on me as it tears off more meat with razor like teeth.

"My name's Arlow." I whisper the introduction with affection tinging my tone. It doesn't acknowledge me at all as it continues to devour its dinner. "Time for your friends."

With care, I cradle the red egg in my palms. The heat of the flames nips at my skin as I push it into the hot embers.

The second one is born just like the first.

It climbs out with more strength than the other dragon. Crimson scales capture the light of the fire in gleaming magnificence. It's just as deadly and beautiful as the other one, but it's not nearly as trusting. I can't even get close enough to offer it a strip of meat without the beast snapping its traitorous snout at me. I toss the food to the floor, and its taloned wing pulls the meat closer. Low growls emit from its throat with every move I make.

"Aren't you a little darling." I roll my eyes at its shitty attitude and begin bringing the last one over to the fireplace.

The white one is a little smaller than the others. It's so pure looking I can't bring myself to toss it into the flames. On my knees, I lean into the fire. I don't release the egg even as the heat stings my knuckles.

The embers crackle as I settle the egg in against the ash and dust.

What if it doesn't do as well? It's so small, what if it isn't ready yet?

I peek down at the two dragons ripping viciously at the last few scraps of meat.

Hell, what if these things kill me before the end of the week?

Life is filled with what-ifs.

You can only leap into the flames and hope you have the strength to walk away from the ash.

Heat washes over me as I lean into the warm fire. The golden hue of the flames glisten against my dark hair reflecting in the shimmering white surface.

Just when my hope starts to sink low in my stomach, a small crack shatters down the curved shell. The cracking sound sparks excitement all through me.

And just like that, another beautiful monster is born.

TWO

SELL-THOSE-FUCKING-DRAGONS-SO-ARLOW-CAN-AFFORD-TO-LIVE DAY

In three weeks, the creatures have grown to the size of wolves.

With the table manners to match.

"Get off the table. You've eaten all the fucking food, Kain. There's nothing else up there for you." I sit up in my bed, glaring daggers at the plate that's laying in broken pieces on the floor. A fuming roar that sounds a little like a pouting cry comes from his red snout, but he continues to search the old table for scraps. New claw marks line the surface of the table that he's currently using as a throne to sit his ass on.

Their names swirled through my sight for days. The names taunted my thoughts. When I finally tested the sound of their names on my lips, they responded as if fate itself named them. It warmed me to give them names. I rarely ever keep and name my creatures. It makes it harder to get rid of them. Just look at the hellhound I haven't been able to part with since I first laid eyes on him.

Don't even get me started on Bobble. I tilt my head at the beady eyes that are looking up at me from my bedside table. As the fish ascends closer to the surface of his glass bowl, its body starts to swell. I think it's a sort of allergy to the air, but it doesn't stop the poor thing from trying to test its limits. As its body bobs above the surface it inflates dramatically, pressing its eyes out impossibly further within its head until I use my index finger to push it back down into the clear water. The fish's body deflates immediately, and it blinks its unintelligent black eyes up at me in thanks. I can definitely understand why Bobble's kind is nearly extinct.

I shake my head at him before looking down at my lap. With anxious hands, I shove at the heavy dragon that's blanketed across my body. Its dark wings are spread across my hips as Chaos lies like a lazy dog between my legs.

Rime is the only good one. He sits quietly in a chair by the window. His gaze assesses every move outside the dirty glass.

He's almost a better watchdog than my actual watchdog. Let's not tell the sweet little hellhound I said that.

A bowl shatters to the floor and my jaw tics as I pin Kain with a hard stare.

"I swear there's nothing left. Get off the table. All that's left to eat is me."

His clawing stomps halt. Silence drops immediately. His head swings my way and he gives me a slow appraisal. Heated, fiery attention skims over my shoulders, my breasts, and the curve of my hips. It's so human-like it makes me pull my blankets closer to my chest.

Chaos's gaze meets mine and a rumbling sound emits from the animal's throat. The humming sound rolls against my core until I kick out of the covers.

My bare feet skim over the warm floorboards. I've slept too late and the sun is high in the sky, heating my little shack to an unbearable temperature.

I'd sleep naked, but the dragons really do seem smarter than the average lizard. Even as I stand here in my bra and underwear, all three of them watch me with too much interest. A groan shakes through Rime's chest before he tears his attention away from me.

I turn my back on them as if they're actual men instead of pets.

I both love and loathe their company. They're sweet and somewhat loyal like a puppy. Adorable even.

But Goddess, are they inconsiderate assholes too.

I slip on a white top that drifts down to my navel and pull on the thinnest skirt I own. It covers me down to my bare feet, but it will also allow the breeze to hit my skin.

"Okay, loves. Who wants to go for a walk?" I shove a smile in place. I even add a hint of happiness to my tone.

I'm making a real effort. It's more affection than I show toward any human.

And it goes very unappreciated.

Their response is apprehensive, guarded glares.

Damn, these things are like a woman when a guy is suspiciously too nice to her.

These dragons don't trust me, but they do defend me. It's an odd sort of combination. When we do go on walks, they're always watching our surroundings and growling when a passerby gets too close.

But they also act that way toward me when it's just the four of us, so I can't really feel too special.

"We're going to take a walk into town. Today is Sell-Those-Fucking-Dragons-So-Arlow-Can-Afford-To-Live Day. Doesn't that sound fun? Festive even, right?" My brows rise, and a wide smile is even passed their way.

Nothing. I get nothing.

All of them tip their heads down to look up at me with narrowed eyes.

"Yes, I knew you shitheads would be excited." I gather three slim chains.

I start with my favorite. "Look at Rime being a good boy." The chain locks around his beautiful, shining, white scales with ease.

I stroke my palm up his slender neck and he leans into my approving touch.

"Good boy." My lips skim his cheek like a favored puppy and his head rests against my shoulder for a moment. A deep rumbling sound, similar to a cat's purr, hums through him.

Yes, he's definitely the favorite. But it's not a tough

competition to win really. He's number one in a competition of dickbags.

Chaos steps closer. He's not the favorite of the three, but he's not the worst either. On my scale of magical creatures, he lingers around affectionate pet and annoying asshole most days. My hands rise to slip the chain around him, and just when I think he's going to make my life easy, he shows me what a true pain in my ass he really is.

The dragon leaps from the bed. His talons pull back, sinking into his skin quickly, and only smooth scales meet my shoulders. I hit the floor hard. The boards groan beneath our weight. Dark, beautiful wings surround me, blocking out the morning light and secluding me with the devious little reptile.

"You fucktile." I groan, my fingers slipping through my hair to feel the back of my head. There's no blood, but pure pain is pounding through my skull.

He hums a rumbling sound. It's cut off immediately as Rime leaps from his perch. He shoves Chaos off of me in an instant, and the two tumble to the floor. Dust billows around them as they snap at one another, lashing out with sharp nails and fierce teeth. Every day they roll around together. Wings and scales in black and white lash out at one another as they playfully try to rip each other's throats out. It's adorable if I'm being honest.

"That's enough. I can't sell a bunch of bloody and scruffy creatures. No one will want you if you're dirty." I sit up as I lecture them, my tone sounding like a complaining mother.

A few more grumbles pass between them before Rime's large wings unveil. With a few strong beats of his wings, he's back at the window. He circles in the old chair a few times before finding a comfortable spot.

I turn to the dark dragon. Chaos' eyes flash with a sort of humor. It's an odd look. A pleased look.

An entirely-too-human look.

A nervous shift has me pausing before raising his leash once again. On slow steps, he comes to me without defiance. His head lowers, and with a steady but hesitant hand, I lower the loose chain around his neck.

His shining scales meet my palm, and I pat the side of his face gently.

"Good boy," I whisper.

Endless, content rumbling shakes through his chest. He's playful. I know that's all it is.

But he's still an asshole about it.

The thin chain rakes across the old boards as I turn away from him. I stand, and with my shoulders squared, I face the real beast. Kain's gleaming eyes narrow on me. A taunting look is in his gaze, and I'm not nearly as confident as I might appear right now.

He sits like a waiting cat. The long sweep of his tail shifts back and forth against my rickety dinner table. With cautious movements, I raise the chain.

With even more cautious movements, he tilts his head back from my advances. A quick move and I've almost got the chain over his sharp, white horns. At the last second, his arm comes up, swiping away the chain in an instant.

My teeth grind together and I all but stomp my foot at his dominant behavior.

"It'll only be for a little while." The tone of my voice is soft and caressing.

Even if I do want to shout and scream at him.

I won't. It won't do me any good.

His wide mouth opens large, revealing every single jagged tooth in his head as he gives me a lazy yawn. He doesn't seem to care at all about my pleas.

I bite the inside of my lip as I try to think of a new tactic.

If we leave right now, we'll be in the heart of the Kingdom at its busiest hour. I could make the most money I've ever made in my life today. I could disappear from my past and my problems once and for all.

Desperate times call for desperate measures.

A casual sway in my hips has my skirt waving across the floorboards. At the few cabinets near the door, I pause and look back at him. His assessing eyes watch my every move with curious attention. Slowly, I open the top cabinet. The rough fabric of my escape bag meets my fingertips, and I pull it down, never breaking eye contact once.

This is my 'on the run' survival kit. If I ever need to leave town, say ... due to a less-than-legal sale of an outlawed creature or illegal use of magic, or if my worst fear comes true and Kreedence finds me, this bag has everything I need to survive until I make it to my next dwelling.

I'm a tamer. I'm a mage. I'm a chick who's got shit taste in men.

But I'm not an idiot.

At the top of the bag is just what I need right now. I pull out the dark brick. It glitters with the sparks of my magic. I save my magic in case he finds me like he promised he would. But I used just enough to make this. I hold the infused item to my chest, just out of sight of the three dragons. My breath wafts over the brick sweetly. That single breath transforms the solid object into a hot and juicy chicken leg. It's golden brown on the outside. Cooked to perfection.

What can I say, only the best for my boys.

I turn to Kain, revealing the delicious treat. The scent of it is enough to make my empty stomach growl.

Gotta keep your eye on the prize, Arlow.

Kain hops from the table. It shakes unsteadily behind him. The three dragons stalk toward me, cornering me against the counter. They all look like they're ready to leap down my throat just to find the source of the food.

I lower myself, extending the food toward the one I have my sights set on. Sharp talons rip the meat from my palm, and before the other two jump in, I lock the chain around Kain's neck.

A long sigh of relief leaves my lungs.

Ugh. That was the easy part. The hard part will be convincing anyone to buy these three assholes.

TAMING

Long claws dig into the dry dirt. The mystical dragons meet the astonished gazes of the villagers. It's something you never really get used to—seeing a rare creature like a dragon. Even I'm impressed with them when I look their way. The men and women halt in their tracks, backing up just slightly to make way for the three dragons who circle my every step. Rumbling growls tear from the dragons' throats each time we pass anyone. I offer the villagers pleasant smiles. No one smiles back.

Honestly, they're used to my shit by now. I may have had a few mishaps in the past.

So a nine headed hydra snake accidentally escaped my cage once. One time. And it didn't even hurt anyone. Let's try to look at the bright side here, folks. Forgive and forget.

Shit happens, right?

"Arlow, I think you've lost your pretty little mind, love." Andrin's dark eyes are held on the creatures.

Their chains clink lightly, and it takes little effort for me to hold on to them. They don't fuss. There's no defiance in them right now. They really would make sweet pets. If only I had the time and money to take care of such beasts.

"I've tamed these three into obedience. They are a true asset to anyone who owns them." Anyone willing to pay the right price that is. I give the shop owner an enchanting smile and he starts to nod slowly.

Andrin knows me. The skepticism in his eyes tells me just how much faith he has in me.

"You'll be going straight to King Barren then?" Andrin and I are both merchants in a way. Except I sell mystical creatures and he sells fresh bread.

Almost the same thing.

As merchants, we both know anything of value will go to the person with the most coin. Unfortunately for me that person is the King; the man who hates my selling ways. So what if I sold him an exploding phoenix one time. *One time.*

How was I to know the thing wouldn't burst into flames but actually combust an entire room? Accidents happen. And my contract states that the buyer is responsible for any and all ... *incidents* after the date of purchase.

Lucky for me, his son adores me. Worships me even.

And he is who I do business with now.

I can't help but wonder if I'd be more accepted here if the Solstice Queen were still alive. No one understands an outcast like a fellow outcast after all. I like to think the Queen from the Northern Kingdom living here in the midlands would have welcomed me.

Or at the very least not ignore me the way the ungrateful King does.

"Yes, by the end of the day the Kingdom of Minden will be three dragons richer, Andrin."

Another slow nod as I pass by his bakery. "Goddess

save the King." His taunting smirk drills annoyance right into me.

The scent of warm bread wafts through the air. My stomach all but cries out for a taste.

"I'll be stopping in on my way back." With my upcoming profit in mind, I make note to visit his business as well as the meat market at the end.

"Well, just make sure he signs the contract. Wouldn't want any more ... *incidents.*" He's still nodding to himself even as my gaze narrows on his dark eyes.

"Incidents happen. I cannot be held responsible for every combusting phoenix."

Just last winter, I sold the Prince my most prized possession: a Minue Quail. A tracker creature that you can't even find in this part of the Kingdom.

I am a true asset to the Prince. He's lucky to do business with me.

"What about that batch of pixies you gave the Prince for his birthday that turned out to have rabies?"

"It was a gift!" I nearly yell the words as I quicken my pace away from his accusing words. Rime rumbles at the insulting man, and for once, I agree with the little creature. "And it wasn't rabies. They were just more feral than I realized." The huffing aggression of my voice dwindles down into a quiet sound of uncertainty.

Rabies. What a ridiculous thing to say. I am a professional tamer. The Prince likes me because I am the best.

And I'm single. That probably helps a little. But mostly because I'm the best.

I'm still fuming over the baker's words when I stalk through the castle gates. The words *Blessed Minden, Saved by the Solstice Queen* swoop into the stone above the gates in proud letters. Two armed men draw their swords on me immediately with their attention held firmly on the purring dragons at my side. Kain's big talons extend when he steps forward and he stares up daringly at the men. Heat and smoke slip through the dragon's sharp teeth as he narrows his green eyes on the guards.

"Prince Linden is expecting me." My chin tips up a little higher and the two men pass quiet looks between them. "I'll wait." I add a casual smile, my arms folding, making the chains clink against each other. I hold a stance of assured carelessness.

One of them backs away slowly. The man before me is tense. Wide shoulders so stiff I can't help but cough aggressively to see how fast he'll react. Very fast in case you were wondering. I have to pull back as the tip of his blade swings up to my apparently assaulting cough.

"Calm down. Just allergies, not venom."

And that's how we're standing as the Prince saunters out. His hands are in his pockets and there's a look of amusement in his eyes that make them shine like emeralds.

He looks like his mother, or so I'm told; the Queen who was loved by all, the one who died too young. People love mysterious, beautiful, and strong-willed women. Perhaps that's why her memory lives on.

Or perhaps it's something else.

"Are you causing problems for my guards again, Arlow?" His warm tone is like a mixture of honey and whiskey. Sweet but strong. It's a sexy sound of someone who's used to getting what he wants.

His entrance doesn't deter his guard's defensive stance in the least.

"I don't know what you mean, My Prince. We were just having a conversation." My index finger runs the length of the blade poised near my lips. "You didn't tell me this one was such a flirt." My gaze flickers to the brooding guard, and he shifts beneath the force of my stare.

Goddess, I love getting out of the house. I forget sometimes how fun it is to play with innocent villagers.

"You were flirting with my friend, John?" The Prince turns his confident gaze to his guard and John finally lowers that damn sword.

"Not at all, my lord."

"Are you saying she's not pretty enough for you, John?"

Poor fucking John.

"That's not what I'm saying at all, My Prince."

"So, you *were* flirting with her?"

John's head lowers and he's quiet for a few seconds. It's just long enough that I feel bad for him.

"I actually brought you something of interest. I didn't come to cause trouble, I promise."

The Prince's gaze rakes down my body, not at all interested in the three pacing dragons at my feet.

"I somehow doubt that very much."

Blond locks fall into his eyes as he takes a step closer to inspect me as if I am the thing he really wishes to buy. Low and menacing growls fill the air between us, and his gaze finally falls to the crimson dragon who's standing protectively in front of me.

"He's cute," the Prince says with a nod to Kain.

Fire erupts from the beast's snout, and he clenches his jaw shut with an abrupt and angry snapping sound.

Yes, he's fucking adorable.

"I've been raising these three for a few weeks now, and I think they'll be ready for battle training in another two weeks when they're a bit larger."

Linden strokes the trimmed hair of his perfectly groomed beard.

He's handsome in that purchased kind of way. He isn't rugged or sexy. He's just ... alluring I suppose. He's so clean and polished it makes me want to cringe away from him for fear of tarnishing his pretty nails.

I don't though. I take an intentional step closer. My arm and hip brush against his smooth navy uniform. His royal and expensive beauty isn't lost on me.

He's not my type at all but did I mention royal and expensive? Yes, he has money and that is what I really need more than any love or affection. Please just give me the coins, and I'll be on my way.

"They'd be impressive assets. When was the last time you've seen a dragon?" They weren't typical along the coast where I lived when I was a girl, but I don't bring up my long-forgotten childhood. Not to Linden. Not to anyone.

"They're rare." He nods.

Rare. Rare is what I always like to hear. Rare like a beautiful and loyal woman. Rare like a strong and fearless man. Rare like everlasting love. Rare like that money you're going to give me that I don't have.

"Indeed."

He's debating with himself in his mind it seems. Why wouldn't he want them? The only downfall is they might accidentally eat him. Or they could make this Kingdom untouchable.

The positives greatly outweigh the negatives here.

"Are any of them female? Female animals are calmer normally. Easier to handle." His curious gaze turns to me and my lips part with a lie before my mind even fully processes his question.

"Of course." I peer down at the glistening scales of the restless creatures. "The black one, without the horns. Only male dragons have horns." Chaos jerks his hornless head up to me. His snout is clenched tightly closed, and I have to force myself to turn away from his oddly scowling look.

I have no idea if any of them are female. They act like brooding beasts, so I guess I just assume they're male, but the Prince wants a female...

Dragons have never been in high supply, but they're nearly unheard of now. Which means their value is going to be amazing.

"The black one definitely calms the other two. The black one and the white one are affectionately playful to one another. They're all very well-mannered, but the black one is such a sweetheart." I run my palm over his smooth scales and, at the last second, Chaos nips at my fingertips.

My hand jerks back from him as I glare daggers at the little reptile.

A real fucking sweetheart, I tell you.

"What do you want for them?" The Prince tilts his head just slightly as Rime begins to pace a slow and stalking circle that makes his shoulders hunch with every step.

"Five hundred parchels. *Each*." And I'll never have to worry about where my next meal will come from. I might hide the rest of my life, but I'll hide in luxury.

The Prince shifts until his chest is skimming my bare arm, his warm breath tangling in my hair.

"What if you give me the dragons today, we make it an even million, and I'll buy you dinner?" Long fingertips skim the inside of my arm and the sound of his rasping tone seems to make all three of the dragons rumble with low and intimidating growls.

I feel the same way, my loves.

A million. What a low-balling asshole.

My palm pushes slowly up his chest, trailing over the shining badges of honor pinned like décor all over his uniform. The way my chin tilts up to his towering height is intentional. Every single thing I do is intentional.

"What if," the smooth tone of my voice has him watching my lips with intensity, "what if you paid me the full one point five, and I'll buy my own fucking dinner?" Long lashes flutter with each innocent blink I give him.

A slow smirk crosses his lips.

"You're impossible, do you know that?"

"I do." There's no sarcasm in my voice. I'm entirely serious about this money.

"What if I gave you half now, half after they've been delivered, and you buy me dinner?" Another step is taken, and his hips are fully in line with mine now, settled heavily against me but not deterring my determination in this deal in the slightest.

Half now, half later, and he gets a bologna sandwich out of the deal.

And I get a lifetime of security.

"It's a deal." I nod and step abruptly back from him and his warming body heat.

His hands raise from his sides as if he's not sure what the fuck just happened.

"I'll wait for John to bring me my payment."

The handsome Prince's face falls as he studies the dirt between us. He looks dejected. Guilt tries to root its way into my stomach, but I shove that feeling aside.

My ex was a handsome man. A deceiving man. I was in love with him. Or at least a form of love. But who he was on the surface wasn't who he was when the world was not watching. And so, I'll live alone. I'll live in poverty. But I'll never put my heart out there again.

Because sometimes, more than just your heart gets broken.

Sometimes, the people you care about most get hurt. Hurting them hurts more than anything else.

"John, John." I beckon the guard over and, on uncertain and slow steps, he dawdles toward us. "John, the Prince needs you to run and bring me exactly seven hundred and fifty thousand parchels." I nod as I speak quickly. "If you could get that in small, spendable bills that'd be really appreciated, John."

John's dark eyes shift from me to his Prince and back again.

"Arlow, I can't just give out that kind of money. The expense will have to be approved. It'll take a day or two at least."

A day or two... I don't have any food at home. I have three dragons who might eat me themselves if I don't have food for them.

"Oh." I bite my lip as my eyes shift toward the ground. "Of course." My voice is tiny and only slightly calculating. "I suppose I'll have to try to search for roadkill along my hike home to feed my little darlings tonight." A short and awkward smile perches against my lips. "It was three miles into town, did you know that? Surely, I can find something on that long journey home, right?" My head bobs with a continuous nod, but I don't give up the act just yet. "The upside is I don't have to worry about being mugged on that long trek back home because I have absolutely nothing to my name. *Noth-ing.*"

Did I lay it on a little strong?

His full lips part and he reaches out to me, but Kain snaps at the affectionate touch before he ever reaches my fingertips. The palm of his hand pulls back as if he didn't intend to comfort me at all.

"Arlow." My name is a long sigh on his lips. "I—I can get ten thousand without question. Let me at least give you ten thousand today. Because we're friends." At the word 'friends' he tilts his head down, trying to peer into my line of sight.

Friends ...

Now is not the time to tell him I avoid friendships and relationships of any kind.

I'll keep that little detail to myself.

THREE

THE TRANSFORMATION

My journey home is a bit more lavish than my hike into town. The royal carriage bumps and bustles, and I sit with my bare and dusty feet kicked up on the navy cushioned bench across from me. I peer past the silky curtain of the back window once again to check on the petite tote there. Ten thousand parchels. Let's repeat that once more, shall we? *Ten. Thousand. Parchels.*

You know that fluttering feeling your heart gets when someone attractive locks eyes with you? That's how I feel right now every time I look at that little tote.

A content sigh slips over my lips and Chaos nuzzles his warm head into my lap. He's sweet when he's tired. My fingers push absently back and forth across the smooth scales of his head and deep purring emits from his throat.

On the opposite bench, Kain and Rime watch the trees pass out the window.

For once, they're being good. They're the good boys I always try to talk them into being.

"I'm going to miss you," I whisper sweetly to the quiet cabin. None of them acknowledges the sentiment, and I shake my head as I roll my eyes at the little assholes.

We stopped twice while in town. An overflowing basket of bread and cake rests near my leg and what is now the tattered remains of fresh roast litters the floor. Kain and Chaos ripped it apart the moment I sat it down.

Perfect.

The ideas of what my future could be begin to flood my thoughts. I've never been able to make it too far. Our Kingdom is enormous. I started on the coast in the city of Warf and five years later I'm just now in the heart of the Kingdom. If I could put space between Kreedence and me, I know I'd finally feel safe. If I could travel farther north, I'd never have to worry about him finding me. I'd never have to worry about anything.

The shaking of the carriage comes to a halt, pulling me from my thoughts. The sleek and glossy door opens, and the footman lifts his hand to me for assistance. Before I can even step out, Kain and Chaos shove past me and run to our quaint little run-down shack.

A tired sigh makes my shoulders slump. I place my hand in his, and the man helps me from the cabin while Rime waits stoically. Only when I look back at him does he leap down. Dust billows around his white scales, but he doesn't take a step forward until I do. He keeps a quiet pace with me, and I keep a slow pace with the solid tote the men carry in for me. The two men give the hellhound lounging near my door a shifting look. Grim's crimson eyes follow their movements, but he doesn't so much as lift his lazy head. I bend and push my fingers through his coarse hair, making his eyes close slowly at the feel of my soothing touch.

I follow behind my money. The King's men set the tote just inside my home, and the moment the door shuts behind the men, I'm already pulling out the money. For a moment, I just let my fingers skim over the neatly stacked parchels. There's an inviting smell that accompanies the bundles of money.

Who knew wealthy had a scent?

Mmm. It smells like crisp paper and long-lost dreams.

I shove harshly at the first several stacks and try my best to push as many bundles into my emergency bag as possible.

Then I struggle to pull the heavy tote across the room. It's weighted despite its small size. It cries with the sound of wood dragging across old boards as I stumble and tug it over to the corner. I pull at the corner floor board, and the loose panel pops free. Rime wanders over to me as I begin the quiet task of stacking up the money in a long line in the empty compartment beneath my floor.

Rime sits in front of me, his head tilting as I work. I look up at him from time to time, but I keep myself busy for the most part. When the money is stacked as high as the flooring, I call it a day and grab the board. I push it in place, but it won't settle back in. My jaw clenches as I shove hard, but the money beneath the board pushes right back.

I huff in annoyance and put all my weight into shoving the flooring back into place.

"Dammit." The curse snaps from my mouth while I fight the little piece of wood.

Dark locks of my hair fan against my lips as I heave in deep breaths.

Rime tips his head low, meeting my eyes, and when I finally focus on him, his scales shimmer oddly against the firelight. My eyes narrow on the glistening tint that's rolling across his body. Right before my eyes, his white scales and wide wings transform in a puff of pale smoke. It fumes thickly around us like a fire smolders somewhere within the animal. Where a curious dragon with beautiful eyes was just sitting, kneels a sexy and incredibly naked man.

"Oh. My. Fuck." My eyes grow wide and my feet try to move, but the most I can manage is to stumble back until my ass hits the floor.

"It'll probably close if you just removed one of the several stacks of money." His pale blond hair falls into his eyes as he nods to me. The sharp lines of his features are entirely serious.

The rumbling tone of his words threatens to steal my breath away, taking my voice and all rational thought with it.

His skin is pale and smooth, casting shadows down

the hard lines of his arms, stomach, and thighs. I force myself not to look at the one part of him that really piques my curiosity.

Shit. Too late.

Goddess, is every inch of this man perfect?

"You're..." Images drill through my mind. Clear images of the pretty white dragon swirling into an apparition of the sexy man who now sits before me. "You're a shifter." I've heard of them, but I've never met one. I just assumed the men who turned to animals were a sort of fairytale. It appears I was wrong.

I can't reveal my magic. Not yet. Very slowly, I reach up, my fingers fumbling until the knife on the countertop is in my grasp.

His crystal-clear eyes drift to the weapon in my hand.

"So, you weren't afraid of a dragon, but a man terrifies you?" His steady tone is filled with condescension.

If he knew the men who had been in my life, he'd understand. Not that I owe this stranger an explanation.

"Animals are kind for the most part. People can be cruel. And men, don't even get me started."

"You tried to sell me an hour ago. Let's not throw stones while you're living in a very fragile glass shack."

My brow cocks at this arrogant man.

Nerves fire through my body as fear trickles in, but I keep my hands steady with a look of total composure.

"The other two, they're shifters too?" I nod toward Chaos and Kain who are ripping apart a loaf of bread on the floor.

"Hey--" He turns his head as he shouts and the other two both tilt their heads to look at him. "--our ... *lovely host* wants to know if you two are just fucktiles like she thought."

Ouch. *Fucktile.* I guess I could have used a more endearing term for them.

Chaos and Kain stalk toward us until they're just behind Rime. In a swirl of red and black, the glistening scales retract from sight, revealing smooth skin. In a matter of seconds, the two dragons shift from beast to man. Their ... manhood hangs directly in my line of sight. My eyes close as I quickly put my hand up before I even see their features.

"Okay, there's an abundance of cock in face right now, and I'd really appreciate it if there was a little less nudity."

Chaos' big hand pushes across his dick, and for an instant, I think he's going to cover himself with his hand. But no. He grips his dick and blatantly adjusts himself. A little piece of me dies inside. And another little piece of me comes to life, I swear it.

"What's wrong with nudity?" Chaos' question demands that I be an adult and look these men in their eyes.

Maintain eye contact. Maintain eye contact. Maintain eye contact.

A shadow of a beard defines his strong jaw. My breath catches when I look at him. His eyes are beautiful. Inky lashes line one amber eye and one sapphire eye, and

I swallow hard at the sight of his intense gaze. The glaring attention Kain gives me reminds me that a question was asked.

"There's nothing wrong with nudity, I just don't want your junk in my face."

Why am I having this conversation right now? Where did my life go so wrong that I'm arguing with my pets about having their dicks in my face?

I should have put my new money to good use and bought wine. I need wine. Lots and lots of wine.

Rime reaches above himself until he grabs the hand towel from the table. Carelessly he tosses it in his lap. It covers his pale skin with the most minimal amount of modesty, but at least the meat market is concealed.

Kain shifts on his bare feet until he spots the nearest cloth. He pulls the thin curtain down from my small kitchen window and holds it respectfully between his lean hips. Light red hair trails down his abdomen and I have to force myself not to follow it all the way down to where the cloth is now held in place.

Okay, two of the three little pigs are now safely within their homes. Not that I'm going to huff and puff and blow anything for anyone.

When my gaze locks with Chaos', he finally starts to get the message. It's not that hard. Cover. Up. The. Dick. Why is it so hard to train these three to do anything?

There's not much in his reach. He stands at Kain's side just near the table. He pauses for a second, the panes of his chest skimming against Kain's before he grabs the only thing on the table.

A glass. My drinking glass. He lowers it until it's perfectly in place in front of his dick. Unfortunately, it's a clear glass and only seems to magnify and warp the image of his cock.

Seriously?

I should have just settled for the one million the Prince originally offered.

FOUR

THE SHIFTERS AND THE MAGE

Kain shoves the other white curtain at his friend and it takes Chaos a second to understand what Kain wants him to do with it.

When the three of them are nicely covered up, I finally really look at them. Kain's hair is nearly as fiery as his scales were. Sculpted lines veer down his body just like the other two men. Though, Rime is a slighter build out of the three. They look like they were built for destruction and power but also beauty and grace.

It's an odd sort of mixture that I've never really seen before.

"You guys can shift back though, right?" I'm mentally trying to figure out how I can present these three to the Prince and still get paid …

"We can." Kain nods, his jaw locking firmly back in place.

Tension lines his body as if he's always one instant away from roaring back into the dragon I know so well.

"Okay..." I take a breath and try to think through all this. What the hell was Agatha doing with three shifters? "I watched you hatch, but you seem to be *very* grown." I blink up at them and force myself not to emphasize what part of them seems the *most* grown.

A smirk tilts Chaos' lips.

"Someone enchanted our dragon form into hatchlings to make us more trusting to anyone who might find us. He wants us to bring him back what he recently lost." Chaos' words are spoken clearly, but they only cause confusion.

A line creases hard through my brow as I try to make sense of the man before me. Someone sent the three of them here to retrieve something he recently lost ... an odd feeling twists through my stomach.

"I've lived here for a while, what are you searching for?"

Chaos looks to Kain out of the corner of his pretty eyes. Kain's lips part slowly as if he isn't sure he'll really tell me.

But he does.

"We're looking for a mage in the area."

Fuck.

That twisting feeling turns so tightly I hunch a little to prevent the pain.

This has to be about Kreedence. My throat tightens just thinking about everything.

"A mage? Mage magic is illegal. The King may have already executed the woman." I speak quickly, filling my lies with all the confidence I possess.

"This one is very much alive. She's young. Beautiful. And very manipulating."

Shit, that does sound like me, doesn't it?

"Hmm." I try my best to feign a look of total innocence. I give them a look like a virgin trying to understand what voyeurism is. Pure innocence, I tell you.

"You know, I have heard rumors about a mage hiding away in a cottage near the river." Sorry Aggie. It's me or you. And it isn't not going to be me.

Besides, she can handle these three.

"Shit, that must be her." Chaos turns his focus onto Kain. Rime does the same.

While Kain just pins me with the most skeptical look. It makes me shift beneath his heated and calculating gaze. He's smart. Too smart.

But I'm pretty. Who are we going to trust here, boys?

My palm reaches out, earning Rime's attention as I bathe him in my comforting affection. Slowly, my fingers skim across his forearm and he watches that movement closely. My gentle touch doesn't have the same effect on him as it does the Prince. He's still just as distrusting.

"I could take you guys right to her." My soft voice has him nodding just slightly.

They really are just like sweet, trusting puppies. I almost feel bad for them.

Almost.

Kain lowers himself, hunching down while holding that small little cloth between his legs. The strength of his thighs demands my attention, and I have to force my gaze to meet his.

"If you're fucking with us—" There's a cruel lick to his words that's harsh but sensual. "—if you fuck us over, I'll kill you."

"Calm down." Chaos shoves at his friend's shoulder. "She just said she'd help us. Don't be a dick."

Kain continues to stare his glaring eyes into mine.

"Don't be a victim to her sweet demeanor, Chaos. Not everything is as innocent on the inside as it appears on the outside."

Well, holy shit. The asshole shifter and I have common words to live by.

"In the morning, I'll run to town and find you three some clothes that cover a little more than your dicks." A smirk creeps across Chaos' face as if he enjoys me talking about their cocks.

In the morning, I'll get their clothes, run by for the rest of the Prince's deposit on these three, and then lead them to Agatha.

It'll be simple. Nothing to worry about.

My stomach turns in disagreement.

"I'm going to bed." I stand slowly, and my gaze lingers on the rows of money left in the tote. "If any of you steal from me, just know there are worse fates than death." A mage could torture them slowly. So slowly death would seem like a blessing.

Not that I can afford to waste my magic right now. Not with Kreedence seemingly back in the picture.

"Steal from you?" A taunting and arrogant look consumes Kain's smooth features. "If I recall, we earned this money."

My lips part as my gaze narrows on the little shit.

"You are not the one on the line who has to deliver the product." And I very much intend to deliver my product.

"That's enough. Everything's fine. We're friends, right?" Chaos starts to tie the cloth around his hips, and I realize this is the second time today someone has tried to force their friendship on me.

"*No*, we're not." I shove past him. The smooth skin of their shoulders sears into my skin as I go.

The cool blankets fling back from my bed as I push them aside and start to climb in. To make things worse, I have to sleep in today's clothes to avoid changing in front of them. I can't even be comfortable in my own home. Perhaps I can talk the Prince into taking the dragons at an earlier date.

Like tonight... Right now.

The bed dips and Chaos' big arms wrap around my hips like I'm a small pillow as he lies between my legs with his head resting on my stomach. My spine stiffens beneath his vise grip, my hands held awkwardly in the air. He shifts, his beard scraping deliciously against my lower stomach.

"Do you know what personal space is?" My whispered words are nearly a shriek.

Kain and Rime settle in on the chairs near the fire, ignoring me and my little outburst completely.

Chaos breathes in deeply, sending warm air fanning against my navel.

"Mmm, not really. You've let me sleep between your legs for months. Don't feign shyness now."

Months? It's been a few weeks. I don't know how time passes for a dragon, but his timeframe is a little off.

His chest is against my core, and all I can think about is if he coughs really hard, I might have an orgasm.

"I think our situations have changed a little bit since this morning."

His head tips up to me, his mystical eyes appearing even clearer in the moonlight.

"You're saying you don't feel safe with me wrapped around you?"

My stomach flutters as he holds my gaze. I haven't had sex in five years. I never really put much thought into that lengthy amount of time. But with this gorgeous man pressed solidly against my core ... I'm very aware of that sad little number.

"That's not the point. I don't even know you and you're already between my legs."

"*Already*, as in you knew it'd happen, you just didn't think it'd happen this quickly." His eyes flash with arrogant humor. My gaze narrows on his taunting smile. "I'm kidding." He sits up a little, resting his weight on his forearms as his thumbs start to sweep across my sides in a way that makes my stomach flutter to life. "Look, our situation is weird. Totally fucked up. But I sleep better when I'm near you, okay? And you sleep better when I'm here, right?"

How does he know that? My gaze shifts to Rime and Kain, but they both seem content to ignore me. The tension in my body eases a little as I start to nod.

"If you want me to move, I will. But don't tell me to go just because society has pushed some unrealistic moral standard into your head about how long it should take to trust someone, to like someone, or to love someone. If it makes you happy, do it."

I lower my hands slowly, brushing my fingers across his smooth shoulders.

He's warm. So warm. And comfortable and sweet. I hate how much I like him held against me.

His familiar eyes and playful demeanor does make it feel like I've known him for so much longer.

"Goodnight, Chaos."

A smile tilts his lips. I feel the curve of that smirk as his head rests against my stomach once more. A rumbling sound of happiness hums through him.

"Night, Arlow."

I try hard not to shiver against the feel of his breath on my skin. My lashes close slowly and total, consuming calm sinks into me as I lie beneath this strong man.

The last time someone held me like this flashes through my mind with the haunting memory of how things ended between us. I shove that thought quickly away.

It's been a long time since I let anyone take care of me.

Not that that is what this is ...

It's just sleep. Nothing more.

FIVE

RIDICULOUS MEN

"Let me deliver it personally." The Prince's words sound like a promise and, for once, I shiver from his spoken words.

Because he just said he'd deliver the down payment right to my house.

This. This is what true love must feel like.

I lean into him with a smile I can't seem to smother.

"That's really nice of you, My Prince."

His chest brushes mine, his gaze skimming down to my lips. "It's my pleasure, Arlow."

The low rumbling growl that fumes through the air has him pulling back just slightly from me. His attention drifts down to the sound of the aggression.

I couldn't bring dragons with me, not when they're walking around on two legs like the arrogant men that they are. I intend to bring home an abundance of money today, and I can't walk the streets without some form of protection.

Hence my sweet little guard dog.

"What—what exactly is that thing?"

Fire rolls off Grim's inky black fur. It matches his blazing eyes that are narrowed on the Prince. Smoke drifts from him like he's burning internally.

And maybe he is.

"This is Grim. He's a hellhound." My fingers dig affectionately into the warm fur between his pointed ears, and his long red tongue licks at his lips.

He's the one constant I've had in my life in the last five years, and he's the one creature I've never been able to part with.

He reminds me too much of a friend I lost. A demon I'll never forget.

A man I'll always love.

"A hellhound?" Linden takes a small step back from me and my pooch.

"Yeah. He's a demon of sorts, so he doesn't eat anything. He's loyal. The sweetest pet I've ever had, really."

It's the one thing Kreedence left me with that I actually love.

Grim is the only thing I care about in my life.

"You have the most interesting creatures, Arlow." He says it in a way that seems like he's reaching for a compliment and this was the best he could find.

"Anyway." His throat clears gruffly. "Tomorrow, I could drop it off personally. If you have time, maybe we could finally get that dinner? My treat this time." The wink he adds at the end makes it hard for me not to roll my eyes.

Prince Linden is a nice man. Really, he is. That's the problem though. He's too nice. And I'm not ready for nice. I wouldn't even begin to understand nice.

But I do want that money ...

Ah, decisions, decisions.

"That sounds ... *nice*."

"Perfect." He leans into me, and I tense beneath his touch as he presses a warm kiss to my cheek.

Another rumbling growl sounds through the air and sharp teeth lash out at the Prince's ankle.

"Grim." The scolding tone of my voice doesn't reflect the relief that's in my heart. "Be nice."

"That's alright. He'll get used to me, I'm sure."

Hmm, that sounds suspiciously like he intends to be around for a while.

"I have to go. I have a couple more errands to run." I wave to him as I stride quickly through the castle gate, rounding the corner so fast the Prince doesn't even have time to reply.

"Good Goddess, why is there an abundance of ridiculous men in my life right now?"

When I was a girl, my mother would buy me pretty dresses to dress my dolls in, and I'd spend the day fawning over how perfect they looked. Today is almost just like that. I hand my naked men their clothes, and I pretend to busy myself with straightening the kitchen, hanging up their dick curtains and such, but really, I'm side-eyeing them hard.

Rime pulls his jeans on, and the waist of the pants hug the smooth curve of his tight ass as he pulls them into place.

A happy sigh slips from my lips.

Chaos tugs the dark shirt down over the hard lines of his abs, and another sound of contentment leaves my lungs.

When I look to Kain, he's staring a hole right through my head.

"Are you done? Or should we make this a strip tease effort for your enjoyment?" Gruffly, he pulls his shirt over his fiery hair, glaring telepathic hate messages with his eyes as he goes.

Why is he so damn moody?

I've been nothing but kind to him.

The fucktile.

"So, lead the way to our mage, and we'll be done with this friendship once and for all." There's no amusement in Kain's voice. The serious tone isn't pleasant or kind. It's entirely demanding.

Right, it's time for them to meet Agatha and hope they accept her as their missing mage.

I have a feeling this is going to turn out really bad either way ...

SIX

THE OTHER MAGE

The journey from my shack to Agatha's cottage is tense, but I refuse to show even a miniscule amount of discomfort.

"Are you three brothers?" I don't ask the question to anyone in particular, but I know there's only one of the three who will actually answer me.

Chaos keeps pace at my side, and he seems to be the least intimidating of their little bunch. Kain has a fiery anger that rolls off him even in his quietness. Rime is an image of innocence with the silence to match. His pale hair is so white, he looks like Jack Frost come to life. Sharp angles and sharp glares define him. He doesn't detach his jaw from its tightly held place to speak one single word of kindness to me.

While Chaos can't seem to shut up.

"We're not brothers. Just a pack of sorts. We owe

someone something. Once we return the mage, we'll be back to our normal life."

Kreedence's cruel features flash through my mind and, before the fear can curl into my stomach, I ask another question to distract myself.

"And what is a normal life for a dragon shifter?"

The setting sun warms the soft dirt beneath my feet. The makeshift road is lined with divots, making a winding path that leads from the outskirts of the Kingdom right to the castle gates itself. Today is one of those days that I used to love. A cool breeze rustles the trees and seeps right into my lungs. Pale colors of pink and white wash out the sky, making the world feel alive and pure.

"Our normal life is—" Chaos' reminiscing words are cut off quickly.

"Our normal life is really none of your business." Kain's arm brushes mine as he keeps his attention on the thick forest.

Well, isn't he fucking charming.

I study him from the corner of my eye before ignoring his shitty attitude.

Our friendship is only temporary. They'll get their mage. I'll sell them to the Prince. We'll all live happily ever after.

"Agatha's is just around the corner here." I pause, trying to think of a way to make this all work out just fine. "Mages, I'm told, are able to manipulate their appearances." That's a lie. You get what you get. Vanity is not one of our strengths. "So, your beautiful mage may not appear as you've been told." Understatement of the year, cough, cough.

Kain doesn't speak. He barely moves his head with a simple nod of understanding.

"Well she can't be hideous. No magic in the world could make this chick look less than what he said. *A modern marvel.*" Chaos has this awestruck look in his pretty eyes.

Huh. I'm a modern marvel, am I? My attention drifts down to my hips and small curves.

As we turn the bend, the trees giving way to an open meadow, the wind pulling at the ends of my long dress, dread drops to the bottom of my stomach.

A small round cottage sits front and center. Did you ever hear those stories about an old witch who eats those kids in the woods?

Yeah, Agatha definitely gives off those eerie witchy vibes.

The visual warnings are all there.

Maybe that's why Agatha and I are the best of friends; we both intentionally keep to ourselves.

Soot stains the small windows in streaking lines that looks like the house itself is crying. There's an assortment of wind chimes near the door, and it won't be until we get closer that the men will be able to realize they're actually bones clattering together; a warning bell of sorts.

Agatha will take care of these interfering men. She'll help me; I just know it.

She's actually one of my favorite people. She's the only other mage I've ever met. She's crazy as hell, but I'll let these guys figure that out for themselves.

I don't hesitate as they start to lag, their steps seemingly becoming more and more uncertain with each new detail their eyes land on.

I pass them a sly but pleasant smile as my knuckles rap gently against the rotting door. My knock doesn't echo or even thud against the thick but damp door. It's more of a quiet sound that Agatha always hears.

My gaze catches on the hole that graces her front yard. I could have covered it for Goddess' sake.

The door swings open and Agatha looks out at me with hazy eyes that drift from my face to Kain, to Chaos, and then to Rime.

She seems to sense all four of us even if she can't visually see any of us.

"Low, welcome. I was expecting a visit from mysterious strangers today, but my sight never told me they'd be so handsome." She has nothing to hide. She knows more than these three assholes will ever understand.

She must know it'll end okay for her. For an instant, I try to pry into my sight. For several seconds, I stand there trying to peer past the heavy veil within my mind to see what our future holds. Shadows and darkness are all that's revealed. Something more powerful is in my future. Something that knows to surround itself with secrecy.

A chill skims all the way along my spine, and the aging lines of Agatha's face turn down in a small frown.

Can she see it?

Can she see what's ahead for me?

I search her unseeing but all-seeing eyes.

"Please, come in. We are all friends here."

Boards creak under foot as I cross the threshold of her small cottage. The moment I enter, darkness surrounds me. The little windows can't seem to allow much light to shine into the cluttered room. Stacks of papers and a hoard of mysterious artifacts tower along the tabletops, demolishing every surface.

She's a collector of sorts. I'm ninety percent certain I saw a shrunken skull here beneath some of these documents at one time, but Goddess knows where it is now. If we were alone, I'd ask her where she found my little darling dragon dicks but now is not the time.

"Which of you is Rime?" At the sound of her question the three men halt just inside the home.

Rime glances toward Kain for an instant. Silence clings to his tightly held jaw. I used to think he was sweet and timid as a dragon. He isn't. He's brooding and calculating with a mask of silence that seems to fester his aggression.

The blind woman turns toward us, giving her full attention as she waits.

And the fucking asshole never once opens his mouth.

I roll my eyes and grip his hand as I jerk him forward. His palm is warm against mine, large and oddly comforting to hold on to.

"This is Rime."

Tension makes his muscles taut. His head turns slowly to glare at me full on. But he doesn't release my hand. He lets me hold on to him despite his hard stare.

Agatha's long gray hair sways as she tilts her head at him.

"You will be the hardest to break, but the easiest to love. The worst to lose." Her words make a shiver race across my flesh, and for some reason, I hold on to Rime's hand a little tighter. "You three think you know so much. So strong, so daunting." She pauses for only a moment. "So stupid."

The smooth muscle of his forearm becomes more rigid as he stiffens from her final statement.

"Enough of the babble. Someone sent us to retrieve you." Kain pushes forward, his shoulder skimming against mine as he holds Agatha's vacant gaze.

Agatha's head tilts just slightly and she seems to study me for a moment. She knows. She knows I brought them here to her to save myself.

"There are other mages in this village, my friends." She looks away from me, busying herself by straightening the mess of papers in front of her. She pushes them this way and that but never really does anything with the stack.

"Where?" Kain's bulky arms fold across his chest, but I don't know why.

"You do realize she can't see your intimidating stance, right? There's literally no one here for you to impress." At the quiet sound of my words, he pins me with his pretty, emerald eyes. A mixture of annoyance and aggression is there in his gaze.

Okay, I'm lying. One person might be slightly impressed ... I'm very impressed with his intimidating stance. Everything from the cut line of his jaw all the way down to the way his biceps seem to bulge against the thin cotton of his shirt.

Yes, color me impressed.

Agatha pulls a small skull from beneath a mound of her treasures. My lips curl at the sight of the tiny animal carcass. Her long fingers glitter from the jewels of her rings as she coddles the little thing, stroking its ivory bone as if it's her favorite pet.

She is an interesting soul, I'll give her that.

"She visits from time to time. But we women of the Goddess stick together." Her head tilts to me. "Isn't that right, Low?"

My brows arch at her accusing tone. Excuse me? I think you've mistaken me for another traitorous mage, Aggie.

"From what little I know of *you women*, yes. That does seem to be a correct statement, Agatha."

Her gaze narrows on me with the look of a disappointed mother staring down at her ridiculously compulsive liar of a daughter.

She's going to hex me right to hell.

"We should go. I'll come back tomorrow and check on you when your poor, dwindling mind is in a better state."

Her lips part with outrage.

"When do you think she'll come again?" Chaos asks when my back skims just slightly against his chest as I try to step away from this tense conversation. I wouldn't say I'm fleeing from this situation, but yeah, I need to get out before Agatha uses her craft to turn me into the sniveling rat that I am.

"Well, if I had to guess, I'd say she might be by tomorrow. Perhaps when my dwindling mind is in a more stable state."

Oh, for fuck's sake, Aggie.

Her unseeing gaze bores into mine, testing, taunting, all but laughing at the hole I've dug myself into.

I take another step back, my arm skimming against Chaos' smooth shoulder. His palm settles against my hip, his touch tingling all through me before he pulls slightly away. The next words out of Kain's mouth stop me in my cowardly tracks.

"Perfect. We'll wait." His chin tips up to the mage but she strikes him right back down.

"You'll wait outside. Unlike some mages, I do not allow strange men into my house." She pauses with a dramatic flair that makes me want to roll my eyes. "Or bed."

Now it's my turn to gape at her.

"So, you're saying if a handsome man like Chaos here asked to slip into your sheets you'd shrug your shoulder at his sexy face?" I blink at her, waiting for her response.

"My sexy face?" His warm words whisper across my skin and I realize I'm still too close to him.

"It's hard for me to say. I can't see his sexy face."

In a flash of twirling papers and rising dust, Agatha is right in front of the shifter. Chaos tilts back from her sudden magical appearance, but he only smirks at the small blind woman. The thin white shawl on her shoulders shifts as she lifts a hand to him.

She looks old enough to be his grandmother.

But when she settles her curious hands on him, she doesn't touch him like a sweet, elderly woman would. No, she doesn't pinch his cheeks even once.

Her palms start at a platonic place on his pecs. Exploring fingers drift down his body, and I can't help but shift, letting my thighs rub together as she touches him the way I've thought about touching him.

His head tilts and he gives me the cockiest smirk I've ever seen. Until her hands drop dramatically lower and she grips his dick in one firm swoop.

The tension in his body jolts from her touch, making her hand slip away.

Kain's lips part and he almost—almost—smiles at his friend. Rime, however, only passes his cruel eyes over the scene as if it is another typical day for him.

"Hmm, well." Her hands pat sweetly against his shoulders. His eyes close tightly as if he's trying hard not to say anything as a smile starts to spread across his lips. I can't really tell if he's trying not to laugh or growl. "Yes, I guess I couldn't really say no. Perhaps I misjudged my weaker friend. I will have to give her my apologies when I see her tomorrow."

"Aggie, you didn't even touch his face." A smirk kisses my lips. Goddess, I want to be her when I grow up.

"I didn't?" Her brows lower over her pale gaze. "Huh, please forgive my dwindling mind."

Her hand pulls away and I can't help but let my gaze flicker to Chaos' hips. Unfortunately, I can't make out the impressiveness that gave Agatha a change of heart.

I guess I should have gotten him tighter jeans.

He turns, big palm pushing across my abdomen, and my body reacts to his touch, leaning into his strong chest as his lips skim against my ear. His coarse beard against my skin sends a hard shiver all through me. "If you're curious, all you have to do is say so, Low."

And just like that, my curiosity is doused with cold water from his ridiculous cockiness.

"Not curious at all. If you'll remember, you're the one without horns." I slip out of his hands and open the door. "Everyone knows dragons are praised for their horns. The bigger horns signal an alpha, a protector, a truly prized beast. You're... hornless. What does that signal?"

His brows lower over his pretty eyes. Just as I'm about to walk out, Rime finally speaks.

"Did she just call you a dickless fuck?"

SEVEN

THE SWEET ONE

The men didn't pry when I stayed a little longer and helped Aggie with her dishes while she napped. Maybe I'm just a good person, maybe the guilt of my lies is eating me alive. We may never know. I waste the day away dwelling on my mistakes and my thoughts as I wash the towering pile of plates. The house is empty and she's still asleep. Or she's ignoring me.

I sigh and carefully make my way around a stack of books that are so tall they're acting as a support beam in the middle of the kitchen. When I close her door behind me, the warm sunlight is gone, replaced with a pale skyline of dusk.

The cool wind catches my dress as I look up at the three of them. Yards into the distance a thick line of tree's attempts to hide the dirt road. There they stand, staring hard at the mage's little cottage. The cool dirt comforts my steps as I walk over to them.

"Rime and I are going to camp out here in case our mage shows up early," Kain tells me.

Well that's pretty unlikely. I'm not much of a morning person. But whatever.

When I don't speak, he continues.

"Take Arlow home. The more we search for the mage, the more danger we're putting her in just by association with us. Women are crazy. She could lash out just to send a message."

Guys, I'll admit I'm a little unstable sometimes, but I'm not crazy ...

Chaos nods, his inky hair shifting into his eyes just slightly. His dark hair and two-toned eyes have this jarring appearance of danger and cruelty, but his personality seems to be a stark contrast.

And before I even get a say in the matter, Kain shifts. One minute he's a brooding and demanding man, the next he's a beautiful, glistening dragon. The smell of smoke tinges the air; it actually crackles with the sound of hot embers. His clothes lay in tattered pieces in the dirt, and I shake my head at his carelessness.

"You guys just think I'm made of money." I stalk forward, picking up a little piece of cloth and raising it to his nose as if to shame the creature.

Kain's snout skims my wrist and he pushes the white remains of the shirt out of his face.

"I'm not buying you new clothes every day." My hands settle on my hips and his emerald eyes gleam as he follows the gesture, studying the curve of my hip a bit too long.

He's so much larger than he was just two days ago. He meets me at eye level now, but I don't let his size intimidate me. Even if his fiery wingspan is larger than life.

"Are you asking us to strip for you every time we shift?" Rime's question draws my attention to his rumbling tone, and, when my attention lands on him, all my snarky retorts drift away.

His fingers grip the hem of his shirt and he holds my gaze as he pulls it off. Etching lines carve his body in solid muscle that makes me swallow hard just from the sight of his perfection. The sharp angle of his jaw tips up in an arrogant way and he wastes no time unbuttoning his jeans.

If I were a classier woman, a woman of virtue and innocence, maybe—just maybe—I'd have the pure heart to look away.

But I'm not.

My heart pounds louder and louder with every small move he makes. He pushes his jeans down so slowly, I'm sure that I'm salivating with anticipation. My attention shifts to Chaos to find him watching his friend with curious attention as well. When the cut, veering lines of Rime's hips are revealed, and then the thin line of hair trails down, so does my gaze. The base of his cock strains against his jeans, and my lips part just as his length and thickness is finally revealed. His erection gives away his emotions despite the always serious look in his eyes. I have to swallow hard and it takes me several seconds to finally tear my gaze away from him.

He seems to always be this quiet man filled with too much pent-up anger. Silence tries to cover his aggression, but it still lingers in the pull of his brow, the turn of his lips, the tension of his pale shoulders. But I don't know why.

He stands before me fully naked and neatly folds his shirt and jeans. It's a casual sort of thing. He isn't trying to be sexy. He just is.

"I'll just give my clothes to Dickless here." He hands his friend his clothes and Chaos' eyes narrow on him.

"Are we sure I don't have horns?" Chaos looks to me for confirmation and a smile pulls at Rime's lips. He looks … manic when he smiles. It's an odd look, like he's not used to happiness at all and he wears it in a cryptic sort of way. An oddly sexy sort of way.

The easy way he smiles makes me realize how close the two men are. Chaos makes him smile without even trying. It's as if he takes away every ounce of anger within Rime and neither of them even notice it.

"You don't have horns, my friend," Rime tells him, clinging to that beautiful but slightly frightening smile. Their fingers brush as he gives him the clothes.

"Maybe they'll show up later when my dragon's at full size. *Or* maybe I'm a grower not a shower." Chaos has a matching manic smile now and the two of them are just smirking at each other like a bunch of idiots.

"I doubt it." Rime bumps his bare shoulder into Chaos' and it's the last thing he says before his image swirls in colors of white and gray and blue.

Frost stings the night air, burning my lungs with each inhale I take.

Scales crawl up his arms, taking over his body at a rapid pace. In an instant, a beautiful and pure dragon stands before me.

I might never tell the others, but Rime is breathtaking in his dragon form. In his human form as well, I suppose. The coarse scales catch the light of the sliver of moon and the stars, and they almost shine with their own cosmic beauty. My palm rises to him, and those calculating eyes watch the movement. When I reach up to him, his head lowers just a fraction, as if he didn't want to, but he can't help but bow to me. My fingers trace across the hard edge of his jaw and that delicious purring sound emits from him. It sinks right into me.

There's this tension between him and me when he's human.

That pressured feeling doesn't exist when he's in his beast form. His dragon seems to want me to want him.

To care for him.

To love him.

"Be careful." It's whispered words that make his features soften, and I suddenly realize I'm becoming too attached to these creatures. I push the sweetness from my tone. "Be careful because I still owe you to the Prince, and I can't really afford to lose that investment, you know." I pull my hand away, keeping my features smooth as he shakes his dragon head at me.

I can't show all my emotions to these assholes.

Goddess knows what they'd do with my little fragile heart if I ever showed it.

Warm fingers slip through mine, toying with my palm before tugging me back.

"Come on. It's getting late." Chaos keeps his hand in mine for a short amount of time as we walk a few feet before pulling away from me.

We trail through the night in silence. The glinting stars through the tangle of tree limbs hold my attention, catching all my hopes and dreams and random thoughts. While Chaos' attention shifts hard over the shadows.

"How long have you lived here?"

His question almost makes me stagger. He's ... making small talk. As if we're friends.

It feels uncomfortable.

"Just a year. I moved around a lot before that." I don't add my sob story about the bad break up and the best friend I lost because of it, or the years I spent trying to adjust. Because we're not friends. Not at all.

He nods, his attention still sifting through the shadows of the thick trees.

"Where were you guys before this?" It can only

benefit me to know more about the men I'm sharing my quiet days with now.

"Uh, it's hard to tell you really. We got into some trouble a few months back. We traveled a lot before that, packing up before life gets too mundane." He tilts his head to me for only a moment, but during that moment his gaze travels the length of my body, making me warm from the small amount of attention.

"That sounds really nice actually. I always wanted to see more of the world." That's what got me in my shitty relationship to begin with. Kreedence offered me a chance to see so much more. Sometimes, more isn't always what you need.

His gaze slowly wanders to the dirt between us.

"You should. Don't settle for what you have. Never settle for less than everything. Life's too short to think you deserve less than all of your dreams and desires."

I cock a brow at his romantic words.

This is the guy they were calling Dickless less than an hour ago ...

Silence settles back in, but his words replay on repeat in my mind. I wish it were that easy. To just accept the things I want and not overthink all the things I need.

Like survival.

Sometimes, the past is too present to really think about the future.

Finally, my home sweet home comes into view. Another board has fallen off the broken window that adorns the front, and it looks like Grim has trampled over the wild flowers that were just starting to grow again.

Speaking of Grim.

Crimson eyes blink into the night. They roam over every inch of the darkness before settling on me like a compass seeking true north. My favorite little demon spawn emits a growl into the night, making hot embers glow as his teeth bare to us.

"It's okay, baby," I whisper as we make our way closer.

His gaze holds firmly on Chaos. A warm hand settles low on my back, my skin tingling beneath the small touch.

"So, this thing's yours?" Chaos' quiet whisper goes very much noticed by Grim. The men haven't officially met my sweet pet. As dragons they've been around one another, but now it feels different.

"He's mine." I try to keep my tone upbeat to tell the little monster that there is nothing wrong.

He was a gift from my ex. The only good thing about that man was this beautiful beast.

"Grim, come here, boy." I lower myself as Grim rises to his full and frightening height. He shadows over me with every slow step he takes.

My hand extends to him, and his head is held very low as his eyes bore into the man at my side. There's a snapping sort of tension in the air. It's accompanied by the low and menacing growl that's shaking through the hellhound.

I start to wonder what he's plotting as he grows nearer, that glinting evil shining in his eyes.

Lucky me, I get to find out.

He leaps, jumping over me and hitting Chaos head on. Enormous paws claw down Chaos' white shirt, tearing right through the cloth.

Another shirt ruined. Just great.

I let out a long sigh, and, before I can even complain, Chaos shifts. An acidic taste meets my tongue as I take a deep breath through the smoky fog of his transformation. Black scales glint against the darkness, his mysterious eyes shine in the night. His roar rips through the shadows, sending Grim flying with one strong push of his talons. And there, lying in a tattered heap on the ground, are his clothes.

"Oh, come on." My whine goes unheard.

The two of them are a lashing blur of sharp nails and fiery growls.

Chaos snaps his sharp teeth at the hellhound. Grim lurches forward and his jaw is clamped down on the dragon's slender neck in an instant. The moment he pulls back, prepared to take another slashing bite, I raise my arm between the two childish creatures.

"That is enough." My words are bit out, my jaw clenched hard as I push my way between the two of them.

Grim sulks back with his narrowed gaze still held on the dark dragon behind me.

"Go lie down." I point to the trampled pink flowers that lay in a demolished mess near my door.

His pointed ears lower just slightly, the only sign that he feels any guilt whatsoever.

When I turn back, Chaos is lying in the dirt. Blood streams down his neck and bare chest. He grimaces, his palm pushing against the slick blood.

I lower myself, trying my best to help him stand as I lead him inside.

"I'm okay." He tells me as I search for a clean towel and dig bandages from my bag. This would be simple to heal if I could just use my powers. I'm actually a pretty decent healer. But I can't.

I can't expose my magic to him.

So, he'll just have to suffer.

When I turn back to him, damp towel in hand, he's right behind me. A rush of air meets my lungs as I try to repress a gasp.

His gaze, one blue eye and one amber, studies me intently as I try to focus on the task of cleaning his wound. Alcohol would really help him, but it's not a resource I have at the moment. I lean into him, very aware of his nakedness. His beard is rough against my fingertips. One palm holds his neck, tilting him just how I need him as I push the cool cloth across his flesh. Gashes cut deep into his skin, barely missing the vein I'm sure the little demon dog was aiming for.

The smooth panes of his chest slide against my arm, his heat flooding me as I try to focus.

The blood coats the cloth too quickly, it's seeping out in gushing waves, but Chaos seems unfazed by the wound. With his attention held intently on my features, I quietly brush a small dose of magic across his skin. It trickles out of my palm in light and unseen waves. I know what it feels like, and I try my best not to use it at full force.

His eyes flutter closed, and he groans low and quiet and lustful. I know it's a sort of warm and tingling sensation, and despite how much I need to save my magic, I can't help but do it once more just to watch his carnal reaction.

Another growling sound of pleasure shakes through him and, suddenly, his hands are gripping my hips. The smooth feel of his erection against my stomach makes my core tighten as I stand there with my hands held caressingly against his neck.

The small amount of energy I used was worth it to hear the sounds of his pleasure.

In the quiet darkness, my fingers trail up the strong column of his throat before settling against his jaw.

He's handsome. His features are carved from stone with beauty that's too alluring to ignore. He really is a predator. Built to attract and built to destroy all at the same time.

For a moment, my attention lingers on his full lips. His lashes flutter open just as my tongue rolls across my lips as I think about every detail of his body that's pressed nicely against mine.

I oddly don't want to kiss him. The thought of it causes a sinking feeling to drop right through my stomach. I don't want to kiss anyone. I don't want sweet sentiments and love. Not at all. Not ever again.

But the hard way Chaos' body is surrounding mine makes me wish I did.

His head dips low and fear strikes through me.

Fuck, he's going to kiss me.

I arch back from him, still holding him and allowing him to hold me but my face is pulled as far away from him as I possibly can.

Confusion darkens his eyes

"I—I think you're okay. It wasn't as bad as it seemed." My hands pull away from him, awkwardly raised just near his face.

He still holds me tightly against him as if he's fighting a primal demand within him.

"Thanks," he says slowly, his grip on me finally loosening before his hands slip sadly away from me entirely.

I turn around, letting out a long breath once he's out of sight but still very much in mind. My fingers slip over the soft kitchen curtain and I pull it away. The cloth is offered to him, and he smirks as he takes it. He wraps it carefully around his lean hips. The golden skin of his stomach demands my attention, but I force myself not to let my gaze linger on his defined body.

I step past him and my shoulders lower as another deep exhale leaves me. The small bed meets my palms, and I push down until I'm comfortably lying on top of the blankets. My face sinks into the soft pillow, and all I want is for this night to be over.

It is very much not over though.

The bed dips low and his big body settles over mine. The air pushes forcefully from my lungs as he hugs his body against me.

"Not tonight. I just want to sleep alone, K."

"K? Is that like a term of endearment?" A weird happy tone fills his words and my stomach sinks.

It does sound like a term of endearment.

Eww.

"I think I'm just lazy and didn't want to put effort into your name, Chaos."

"How endearing." His big palms slip around me as his head settles low against my back. The trimmed beard makes my spine arch against the tickling feel of it.

We're opposite of how we normally sleep. Instead of his hands pushing against my spine, they're pushing between my hips, and I can't help but shift against his heavy touch. His fingers tense against the sensitive skin between my hipbones, so low but not low enough. With a breath caught in my lungs, I wait for him push our boundaries, to skip the heated looks and teasing touches and slide his fingers right where I want them.

Big hands flatten against my navel, no longer sweeping against my flesh in a tingling torment that makes every fiber of my being ache. Warm lips whisper against my lower back as he brushes a chaste kiss over my spine. A shiver shakes through me.

"Good night, Low."

The tension in my chest slips away on a heavy breath.

"Good night, K."

A rumbling sound of amusement hums through his chest and against my back, and I think about how good he feels wrapped around me until I finally fall asleep.

EIGHT

RECKLESS EMOTIONS

I slip out from beneath the sweet dragon before dawn even strikes the horizon. It only takes an hour of my time to run my errands this morning. Once again, I buy a couple pairs of jeans and shirts for the guys, but then, before I head home, I make one more stop. Grim saunters toward me as I trail up the worn path to the front door.

"Good morning." I can't help but always talk to him like a person. I probably talk to my little hellhound more affectionately than I do other people.

His soft fur meets my palm as I push between his ears, and he hums an approving sound. The warmth of his body skims against my legs as he leans into me before I slip inside. Bright lines of sunlight cast across the old boards and Chaos lifts his head from the blankets as the door clicks closed behind me.

"You left?" Confusion lingers in his eyes. "Without

me? The whole point of me being here is to protect you from that mage."

Aww. He's trying to protect me from myself. Good luck.

"I got us breakfast." I easily ignore his frustrated tone and the mention of food seems to be the perfect distraction.

He holds his curtain in place around his hips as he slowly makes his way toward me.

"What'd you bring?" The checkered cloth on top of the basket is pushed away as he peeks inside. His lips curl slightly. "Grapes? You got us grapes."

I take a look myself, making sure I got everything I asked for. "And apples."

His pretty eyes search mine as if this might be a cruel joke.

"I—I'm a dragon, Low."

Wow. He's playing the dragon card right now.

"Oh. I assumed you were a man too who needed more than just meat to survive. I guess I'll just eat this myself."

His fingers grip the edge of the basket as I start to pull it away.

"No. No, grapes sound—" His voice cuts out slightly like he can't bring himself to say it. "That sounds really good. Thanks."

A small smile pulls at my lips. It makes me happy that he's willing to eat something he obviously doesn't like just because I got it for him.

I pull out a chair at the table and he takes down two white plates for us. The ones with the chips and cracks in them. The only ones I have. But he knows exactly where they are.

Because, in his head, he's lived here for months.

"What's dragon years compared to human years?" I cut an apple for us and divide it out on a plate as he steals a grape and pops it into his mouth before sitting down.

"Um, I don't know. I'm twenty-five, but my dragon feels older. Wiser. If you can believe that." He winks at me and smiles even more when I roll my eyes at him.

"That *is* hard to believe." I nibble on a slice of apple as he puts the whole thing in his mouth and chews approvingly.

"This is really good."

I can't help but smirk. It's just an apple, but he's sweet enough to show his appreciation.

He's different from the other two. Less guarded.

"How long have you guys known each other?"

His gaze shifts to the sunlight outside, and I wonder if he'll cut our small talk short and avoid my prying questions.

"Since we were kids. My mom and Kain's mom grew up together; therefore we grew up together. Brothers by bond, I guess. We met Rime when we were teens. He's from the north originally. When we met him, he … was alone. A lot in his life. And it showed." A sigh skims from his lips like he doesn't want to say more but he wants to explain too. "Rime isn't good with trusting people. He's never had to really. While Kain and I grew up as playful children, it was safer for Rime to grow up … as a dragon. He was alone, and to protect himself, he rarely ever shifted into his human form."

My brows arch at his words. Rime's more beast than he is man. How terribly sad. I'm not the same, but I do know what it's like to be alone and afraid.

What happened to him to make him so distrusting?

"I can't imagine not having at least a family." My lips part as I realize I said those words aloud.

Chaos steals another slice of apple, his fingers brushing mine just slightly.

"Well, that's not true. He has us. We're a family. The only family that matters. Among all the bullshit of his past, he has us."

I nod, trying to push out the pressing feeling within my chest.

I'm—jealous in a way.

My family was there for me, but they never embraced me as a mage. They always hid me away because it was safer. The powers within me, and my emotions in general, suffered because of it.

I shove away that pitying feeling and choose snark instead.

"What's Kain's excuse then? Why's he so damn charming?"

Chaos' lips quirk into a smile that makes my stomach tangle, and my gaze clings there for a moment too long.

"Kain." A humming noise catches in his throat, his attention held on the way I'm pushing the last bite of my apple into my mouth. "Kain is a mess. He's been hurt too much for him to be as happy as he should be."

He's been hurt? He's so handsome and strong, I can't imagine anyone hurting him. But I know what it's like to be hurt and to hide it.

"And you're the stable one of the three? Carefree and full of happiness."

His gaze holds mine, shining with color and life and energy that seem to buzz between the two of us. There's a sadness there in his amber and sapphire eyes that seems to tear away the happy feeling leaving me with a twisting sensation of guilt.

"I guess." He shrugs before standing, taking the jeans and striding away from me before he pauses for only a moment. His next words are spoken so low I barely hear his quiet confession.

"Or maybe it's just easier to pretend."

My arms fold across my chest as we wander up to the tree line we left Kain and Rime in. The thick branches overhead shadow over the two dragons. The moment I'm near enough, they shift in a swirl of red and white like winter snow mingling with fresh blood.

I'd like to say that I'm used to their nudity by now,

but I might never be. I do applaud myself for pretending not to acknowledge their dicks.

"She show up yet?" Chaos nods to Kain.

"I doubt it."

Three sets of confused eyes land on me, and it takes a moment longer for me to realize I said that sarcastic remark aloud.

"I mean, *obviously* she hasn't."

I avoid their narrowed eyes, and instead, I peer past them, meeting Agatha's vacant gaze. She stands in her small front yard, staring directly at me. We're concealed here. Completely out of sight within the forest, but it doesn't stop the intelligent mage from keeping tabs on us.

"Morning, Low." She waves as if she's all too aware of the four of us lurking in the shadows. "That bitch show up yet?" Her voice sounds frail against the curse word, and it takes everything in me not to smirk at her fond new name for me.

I suppose I deserve that.

"No, she hasn't. No sign of her yet." I yell back to her.

She nods as she picks a plump tomato off a vine and adds it to her basket.

"Well, I'm sure she'll turn up." She ignores us as she pulls another nice round tomato from the vine.

Kain's eyes narrow on the old woman as if he might tackle her to the ground and demand information from her.

I roll my eyes at how ridiculous my life has become lately.

Talking about myself in third person to my only friend in life. Prancing around in plain sight while I pretend not to exist entirely. I'm just digging my own grave really. But I can't leave until I have the money.

"I brought you a snack."

Rime and Kain both turn to me with rapt attention until they see the two apples in my hand. Once more, I'm met with scowling glares.

It's like these assholes have never seen an apple before.

"It's not going to kill you to eat fruit, I promise."

Rime snatches the apple from my hand, his fingers skimming against my wrist before he takes an enormous bite.

"I'll eat basically anything." He doesn't look at me as he chews, staring out at the dusty yard in front of Agatha's cottage as if he might have missed his mage in the ten seconds it took him to engage with me. His teeth sink nearly into the core with another large and careless bite.

Kain slowly takes the other apple and with less enthusiasm, he takes a small, slow bite. Sunlight shines on his fiery hair making it brighter, making his forest green eyes darker, making him entirely too attractive for his own good.

But it doesn't distract me from noticing that I received zero thank-yous for thinking of them.

Of the three dragons, it's easy to see Kain is the leader. The alpha. It's like he carries the weight of their problems on his shoulders and he watches out for them even if he doesn't realize he's doing it. I wonder what it'd be like to always have someone on my side like that.

"Everything okay at home?" Kain turns to me, and I realize I'm still studying the curve of his jaw when he tilts his head down to meet my gaze. "Everything okay?" he repeats slowly.

"Yeah. Perfect. Nothing to worry about."

He shakes his head, his hard gaze shifting over every shadow.

"Good. We'll take care of this. I—I'm sorry we dragged you into this." The sincerity in his voice makes the guilt within me rise to an unbearable high, threatening to drown me for deceiving these innocent men.

The tightness in my chest doesn't allow a single word to slip past my lips, so I nod instead.

"Take her home. Take care of her. If anything happens, just let me know." Kain taps intentionally against his temple, and my brows lower as Chaos slips his hand into mine. I'm still watching Kain when Chaos starts to lead me away, back the way we came.

Fierce emerald eyes lock on mine, holding my gaze until I'm completely out of sight. I feel Kain's attention burning across my flesh even after the silence and peace starts to settle in.

"What did he mean when he tapped his head?"

"You're a curious woman. Take it from someone who knows, nothing good comes from too much curiosity."

His words only make me more interested, about him

more than anything. Chaos is the tallest of the three, well over six feet tall with the solid muscle mass to match. He's unexpectedly sweet and gentle despite his bulky exterior. It doesn't surprise me to know he's a curious creature as well.

"I'm a beast tamer. It interests me."

"So, you like to study us? Is that why you're always checking Kain out?" He pauses for a beat. "I always thought Rime was the pretty one." His shoulder bumps against my bare arm, his hand still loosely holding mine. The teasing lilt of his voice makes me smile but the honesty in his word circles my mind. He thinks Rime is pretty …

He's not wrong.

"I studied animals for years actually."

"You're good with animals." His tone becomes serious but quieter. "My dragon side loves you. He'd try to steal you away for himself if I let him."

Dragons are greedy by nature, but his comment has me openly gaping at him. No one's offered to steal me away in a long time.

I'm older now. I don't need someone to save me from my life.

Not that I'm doing such a spectacular job on my own.

"In our dragon form, there's a bond that can be made. It's so intense our thoughts and emotions link together."

"Like telepathically?"

His lips part as he thinks through his thoughts.

"Kind of. It's typical for a family to speak between

themselves within their minds. Kain and Rime and I have been together so long we just synced up. It's even stronger for mates."

Mates. An intense love that syncs creatures' minds, bodies, and souls. My heartbeat kicks up a gear at the sound of the serious word. I wonder if he's ever felt that.

I'm bordering on information overload but I can't help myself from learning more about him.

"Have you ever mated with someone before?" I try not to look at him as I ask the personal question.

His lips pull up into that half smile he always has. That sexy look that demands my attention.

"No. Dragons want to mate for life. Doesn't always happen. It almost happened for Kain." His mouth snaps shut as if he wishes he could take those words back.

Intrigue swirls through my mind, but I can tell he isn't going to say more about that topic. Is that who hurt Kain? My stomach twists at the thought of someone hurting him.

"What about you?" His attention swings to me, hanging on my words before they're even spoken.

Sinister's name circles my head on repeat, sending my emotions into a frenzy of confusion and sorrow. He was my best friend.

And the years have passed so slowly I'm not even sure of what my own feelings for him were anymore.

"No. Not really." I hate that I just said that. But it's easier to say I never loved him than to explain the mess of a life I've led.

Falling in love with my ex-boyfriend's brother isn't something I advertise. Saying I ruined his life and mine sounds pretty terrible. Telling someone I'm on the run from said ex-boyfriend also isn't exactly something I want to share. Especially with the man who's currently holding my hand and sending me shy smiles that start to make my ovaries plot what our future dragon shifter babies would look like.

Why am I such a mess?

"I find that hard to believe. You act like you've had your heart broken. Destroyed." Another small smile is passed my way.

Ignoring his entirely too correct statement, I look away from him.

This feels like a date... All of this. Every bit of being with Chaos feels like romance threw up all over my day.

I hate it.

I love it.

I hate that I love it.

My hand pulls away from his warm touch, choosing to fold my arms across my chest instead. For the rest of the day we walk and talk and I don't even realize that we're just roaming around as an excuse to get to know one another. It's odd but he makes it so simple. Everything about Chaos is this easy feeling that I haven't felt ... possibly ever.

The day slips away.

We make our way down the little dirt path that leads up to my shack. I'm going to miss this shack when everything's all said and done. After I collect my money, or once these three find out I'm the mage they've been looking for, I'm going to miss this place.

Grim stalks toward us, his bushy tail wagging as he strides toward me. He gives a low growl of a greeting to Chaos before planting his paws on my shoulders and swiping his tongue across my cheek. He's so much larger than I am in this stance. He shadows over my body.

"Did you miss me?" My fingers push through his hair, singeing my fingertips just lightly but not enough for me to not show him some attention.

At least he isn't trying to rip my new lovely shifter friends to pieces today.

Chaos raises his hand as if he might pat the hellhound as well, but Grim snips at him, baring his teeth like Chaos just tried to take away his favorite bone.

"Good to see you too." He shakes his head at the beast before pushing open the front door. Chaos walks through the front door of my house like he's lived here his entire life.

I pat Grim's head once more before trailing after the shifter.

My shoulders sag slightly as I look up to the sun that's attempting to fade down into the evening sky, casting pale light across the horizon. Exhaustion hits hard the moment I close the door behind me.

And I run right into a solid chest.

Chaos's fingers grip my hips, tensing into the flesh of

my lower back as my palms settle on his shoulders. Why am I always in this man's arms?

"I was going to make some dinner." My voice is husky when I speak, and his gaze follows every syllable that skims over my lips.

"That sounds good." The sweet demeanor he always holds isn't there anymore. A dark look that I can't quite place is in his eyes.

A beat passes and it takes too much effort for my fingers to release him, my palms trailing down the curve of his biceps before finally falling away.

Logically, I know how awful it would be for me to become too attached to any of them. The more time I spend with Chaos, the more I forget that logic entirely.

I keep my mind busy as I stuff already baked bread into a pan and begin to press cheese and herbs into the center. The heat of the fire is barely warm as I place the food over the embers. I stay there, seated near the flames, and keep my attention safely held on the fiery coals.

"What the hell is this?" He pokes Bobbles head and the fat little fish submerges below the water, deflating the moment the water covers his white body.

"That's Bobble."

"Bubble?"

"No, Bobble. He's a tumid fish. The air seems to make him swell up to a life-threatening size."

His dark brow arches as watches the fish bob right back to the top, his scales stretching as he blows up so much his face presses against the glass, his beady eyes pleading for help.

Another push of Chaos' finger sends the fish back into the safety of his bowl. "He's ... not very bright, is he?"

I shake my head.

"He's sweet though. He just needs a little help in life."

Chaos passes the fish a worried look as he walks across the small room.

"What will you do with all this money?"

He leans against the small counter near the kitchen window, his gaze fixed on me, his features shadowed in the dim lighting.

"I guess I'll travel." Run away is more like it. I'll run away for a final time. Far away where my demons will never find me.

"Not going to visit family? A boyfriend maybe?" His hinting words are serious. It seems to be the first completely serious thing I've ever heard him say.

"No boyfriend. My family—" I think about my mother and father who live on the other side of the country. They're safer there. My mother is older and it's easy for her to hide her magic. She's content to let it disappear entirely.

I'm not.

"They live along the coast." My lips part as I realize how honest that statement was. I'm telling him too much.

His brows rise. Coastal life is more luxurious, and everyone knows it. The coast is lined with towering tropical houses, beautifully painted and nicely kept up. The imports there and the seafood are sold at a fair and impressive price to the in-landers. My father made a name for himself selling ships.

I miss him. I miss my parents.

"It's beautiful there." His response is quiet and surprises me slightly. It's a safe thing to say. Instead of prying, he chose to make a statement that everyone can agree with.

"It's amazing there." It's like this place that I haven't seen in years where the water and the heavens meet, tangling together into this beautiful and untouchable horizon.

I pull my knees to my chest, locking my hands around my shins as I wait for the cheese to melt into the bread.

"That smells really good." The boards creak as he comes closer. Slowly, he lowers himself down beside me. The smell of warm smoke and timber and something completely Chaos washes over me.

"Thanks."

"I think deep down you like taking care of us fuck-tiles." His arm brushes mine as I turn to glare up at him, a smile trying to pull at the thin line consuming my lips.

"Hardly. You three are more work than you're worth."

To be fair, they're worth over a million parchels, so that's definitely the biggest lie I've ever told in my entire life.

"You'll miss us when we're gone. Admit it." His

shoulder bumps against mine, teetering my balance just slightly.

I hum for a moment and the sound of it seems to draw him closer. When I look up again, his head is tilted toward mine, his mouth just an inch from the smile upon my lips.

"Yes, I'll definitely miss my pain in the ass dragons when I'm out living a luxurious life."

His lips pull into that half smile, and as he leans closer, a mixture of want and terror rips through me. Goddess, do I want him.

But at the same time, I want nothing to do with that reckless want.

I look away from him. My gaze holds hard on the flickering flames kissing against the metal of the bread pan. The rapid beat of my heart thunders through me as I try to catch my breath, busying myself with removing the food from the fire.

When I stand with the food, Chaos has already set out two plates, and the moment I sit the pan down at the center of the table, he starts cutting into it. The blade sinks into the soft, cheesy bread and it takes me a moment to realize my sweet dragon is serving me.

"Sit down." His command is a whisper against his lips.

And I obey.

I sink into the small wooden chair and he slices a large hunk of bread off for me. Strings of cheese make a line between my plate and the pan, wafting a strong and delicious scent all around us.

"Shit, this smells fantastic." His compliments shower around me, flooding me with more emotion than I've felt in years.

His appreciation always seems to catch me off guard, making me forget my breath and voice. He isn't nearly as fierce and intimidating as he looks.

"Thanks." The quiet word disappears right off my tongue in a whisper that I can barely hear.

What the fuck is wrong with me? Why are all these feelings drowning me right now?

I tear a small piece of bread off, and the moment it touches my tongue, I hum as the flavors fill my mouth. I don't cook much. There isn't much food to cook usually. Even this isn't too fancy. But it's good.

"It's good, right? My girl's a good cook." His arm bumps mine in a playful way and it takes me a moment to realize he just called me his girl.

Chaos is confusing. Alluring and charming and confusing.

In a weird, very strange way, I think he's just overly friendly. All the small teasing brushes of his arm against mine, the compliments, the new possessive nickname, it must just be how he was raised. I bet his mother is proud of him.

She should be.

His Adam's apple works as he swallows a big bite of food before devouring the rest like the animal that he is.

Yes, he's a total gentleman.

I have got to stop appraising him. He needs to stop complimenting me, and above all else, I need to remember that he and his friends are basically hunting me.

"I think I'll go to bed early." I stand and quickly deposit my plate in the sink. My behavior is off the wall, I know, but my heart's pounding a mile a minute while fear of being caught starts to twist my stomach. It's all very hard to think through.

He doesn't have time to reply as I quickly move away from him before I lie down. My arms hug my pillow beneath my head as I bury my face into the soft material, attempting to block out the bright evening skyline.

It's too early for bed, but it's the only thing I can do to avoid the man seated at my kitchen table.

I just have to make it a little longer. I just have to keep my eye on the prize. I just have to keep a wall between me and these three shifters for another day or two.

A suffocating feeling of anxiety starts to push within my chest.

The bed dips, dropping my stomach right along with it. A strong body wraps around mine, his palms pushing low against my abdomen with a trail of heat.

"Chaos can you please. I can't—I can't think, and I just want to sleep, and I'm tired, and I hate how good you feel." My mouth snaps shut but it doesn't stop the words I've already spoken.

I tense beneath him. Seconds tick by as we both process what I just said.

Why did I say that?

"You feel good too." His words tingle into me in a delicious way. "My mind is always split. There's this rational human side of me, and then there's this primal dragon side of my thoughts." His low tone drifts right through me, and I can't look at him. I force my face deeper into my fluffy pillow to avoid the confessions that are growing in the air. "My dragon side is demanding."

The words he said earlier swarm my mind. He said his dragon loved me ...

That thought both terrifies me and warms me all at once. His fingers tense against my stomach before slipping lower. His touch burns over my skin, making energy course all through me with every slow move of his fingertips. My lashes flutter as he cups my sex from over the thin material of my skirt, and a heavy sigh falls from my lips.

The tingling feeling in my core tightens. My hips skim against his palms, my ass rocking hard against him until he finally shifts higher to meet me just right. The pillow sinks and his hand plants near my head just as his cock grinds against my ass.

A repressed sound leaves him and fans against the back of my neck. It takes a second before I start to meet him. Our hips rock hard together but only in a way that truly benefits one of us. His lips press to my messy hair, and I keep my face tilted away from him as his mouth skims against the curve of my neck. His beard brands my skin in a tingling delicious way.

The warmth of his palm sears across the back of my thigh as he pushes my skirt higher and higher. The thin material teases my skin and my legs part wide for him as he settles in; his chest brushes against my back with every move he makes.

He feels good. I love the way his hands feel against my skin. I want his mouth on my body. I want to feel every inch of him. For a fleeting instant, I consider turning to him. I consider kissing him deeply just to know how he'd taste.

But I don't want that connection. I want the building release to come crashing down. I want him to fuck me hard. But I don't ever want to feel that soul-crushing emotional attachment to anyone like I've felt in the past.

My palm pushes at the hard length of his cock behind me and he thrusts against my touch. I shove blindly at the waist of his jeans until smooth skin meets my fingers.

I shift my hips for him as he pulls my underwear down. When his palm pushes over my center, a whimpering gasp slips from my lips and the sound is silenced against the soft pillow beneath me. Slow and deliberate strokes guide his fingers up and down my slickness. He rubs hard against my clit, and a shaking breath fans across my hair, my eyes slipping closed. One finger sinks in and then another, and he groans against my neck before kissing me there tenderly.

Shamelessly, I grind myself against the firm movements of his palm until I'm moaning from the feel of his hand working my body.

"Relax, Low. I'll take care of you, I promise."

I don't have time to realize how quickly he intends to fulfill that promise.

His palm slips away, and with my chest heaving, I look back at him with a needy look that makes him smile. The evening light strikes across the dark stubble of his jaw, making his smile appear more dangerous than I've ever seen it.

Big palms grasp my hips and he pulls me against him until every hard inch of him is slamming into me at once.

He uses me as he strokes himself hard, stretching the deepest parts of my body until I'm crying out from the rough feel of it. My orgasm builds and tightens within me as he thrusts deeper and deeper. I'm spread beneath him, his nails digging into my skin as he fills me completely from behind. The dominance of his body over mine sends a rush of energy right to my sex, and I rock forcefully against his every thrust.

It's like nothing I've ever felt before. Chaos is this surprising combination of aggression and care that I never expected.

The warmth of his palm skims up my spine in a gentle caress. His fingers grip the base of my hair and he pulls hard until I'm bowed beneath him. His grip tightens with every hard thrust. My gasps and moans fill the silence, and every sound I make seems to fuel him on. It's this delicious mixture of pain and pleasure. His dominance excites every part of me, but I also want him to know he doesn't own the control between us.

I arch against him, settling against his thighs as his chest melds against my back. My spine bows until my hands push through his hair. My hands are above my head, gripping his locks tightly as he rocks his hips harder.

"Fuck, Low." He releases my hair and I release him, both of us relenting to one another. The cool mattress meets my fingertips once again as I settle my chest against the blanket. My palms fist the sheets. He groans, his thrusts becoming jarring and hard, but he doesn't stop for even a second.

Heat sears over my skin as his palm skims across my hip before drifting lower. His fingers push down my sex, slipping against the base of his cock before sliding back up. Fast and hard circles press against my clit in the most demanding way. The energy within me coils tighter, and I bury my face in the pillow as I scream his name.

My release shivers all through me. It draws him in deeper and he slams in one more time, his nails raking across my hip as he stills behind me.

His heavy breaths shake through the silence, and the pulsing of his dick makes me tremble beneath him.

Neither of us speak for a long moment. Finally, I turn, letting him slip from me to face him. He's the first person I've slept with in five years.

Goddess, that was the best decision I've made in five

years, I guarantee it. I'm mentally applauding my good choices in life.

I think I might even miss him, and his cock, when I sell him off to the Prince.

Hesitantly, his fingers push over mine before he holds my hand lightly above my head. He holds himself above me, studying me. We stay like that for several quiet moments.

"I –I haven't had sex in a while." His quiet words make me smirk. His eyes close slowly before he smiles. It's an awkward statement that makes my heart stumble. "I just meant ... I didn't mean for it to be rough. I—"

It was so perfectly rough.

"Shut up." A smirk hesitates against my lips. I've never seen him so adorably awkward before. "Do you want to try again?" I cut him off before he can say sorry because that's literally the last thing I want to hear in bed.

"Fuck yeah, I want to try again." His gaze trails over my features and he leans into me, his attention held on my mouth.

At the last moment, I turn away. Confusion crosses his features and my heart starts to pound unsteadily. Instead of letting him kiss me, I lean into him and push my lips against his warm neck. His salty taste meets my lips, and I rake my teeth slowly across his skin until he settles his hips against mine.

The tip of his dick sinks slowly and gently into me, and I gasp from the feel of it. Long and slow thrusts fuel his movements. He takes his time drawing out my every shaking breath even as his fingers tightens against my wrist.

It's meticulous, and careful, and gentle, and so fucking slow I feel like I might come all over again from the tormenting pace.

He's very much *not* dickless. I guess I just had to find out firsthand.

"Fuck." I can't form a real sentence to save my life, but my gasping words keep coming from my mouth with every thrust he gives me.

At the sound of my approving words, he drags his length slowly across my sex before sinking deep over and over and over again.

Our breaths and my moans echo around the small room.

My climax rises, and just before I come hard against his cock, a hesitant but firm knock shakes against my front door.

He stills above me, his shoulders tensing beneath my touch, and I almost cry out from the sudden halt.

"Don't stop, please." It's a gasping plea as I rock my hips against him, desperate for that feeling to return to me.

But it's gone.

And he isn't moving.

And whoever the fuck is at my door had better be important.

I shove out from beneath him, pushing my skirt down

as I trail over on unsteady legs. My chest is still heaving as I open the door.

The cool night air meets my sweaty skin, and, to my unfortunate luck, it *is* someone important.

It's the Prince, here for our date.

Fuck.

NINE

IGNORING REALITY

"Are you alright? You don't look well." The Prince's pale brows lower over his shining eyes.

With another heaving breath, I force a smile to my lips. My hand shakes just slightly as I push my tangled hair down into an almost manageable state.

"Yeah." The breathy tone of my voice sounds like sex itself. His gaze flickers across my flushed features.

Worry and embarrassment start to sink into me. I wasn't loud. Let me rephrase because it's been five years, and I might have been just slightly loud, but I wasn't *that* loud.

Was I?

"Okay." He nods but his posture is a tense sort of stance that makes me question what's going through his little royal mind. "I brought your payment." He motions for the two men who are holding an absurdly large and intriguing tote between them. Two more boxes weigh down the back of the shining navy carriage.

Payment. Yes. Excuse my shit manners.

"Please come in." I step aside, and just when he's about to enter, logic creeps right up on me and reminds me that there is a very naked man in my bed. "Wait!" I throw myself against him, blocking his path and making the two men behind him stumble, dropping the precious tote to the ground. "Be careful back there," I say with concern, leaning on the tips of my toes to peer past the Prince.

"Can we come in...?" Thick brows lower even further and I can't help but wonder how furious he'd be if he found Chaos.

Prince Linden is a friend. Kind of. An associate of sorts. But I know he likes me. And I also know he has a terribly fragile ego that constantly needs to be stroked.

How furious would he be to find out I spent all these months ignoring the advances of the most prominent man in the Kingdom just to fuck a dragon?

Goddess, where did my life go so wrong that this is a real question for me? A moment ago, I was so pleased with my good choices in life, and now I'm starting to second-guess those fantastic decisions.

How do these situations happen to me?

"Um—" Just before a lie has a chance to slip over my lips, a purring sound of fire and lust reverberates against my side. Chaos' snout pushes beneath my arm until my hand is against the back of his neck.

His curious eyes settle on the Prince before me. Narrowed slits of glowing attention is held on him.

"Wow, he's incredibly tame." Linden's brows rise a little higher as Chaos nuzzles closer.

And closer.

Until his face is nearly pushing against my breasts.

"Okay—" I shove the beast back from me, "—that's enough." My lips purse and a humming sound shakes through him.

I step back, my gaze held on the dragon as the Prince and his men usher my earnings into the room. The shack looks smaller now with the totes filling the majority of the kitchen floor. Not that I care. I'd climb in there and live with that money. And what a happy life I would live in there. Surrounded by all the things I care about in this world.

"I'm sorry I'm so late. Work always gets in the way." He takes a step closer to me, and I'm very aware of his men exiting, closing my door behind them.

Until he and I are alone.

He and I and one big fucking dragon that's glaring daggers at the close proximity of the Prince. His fingers slip through mine, and I force a pleasant smile to my lips.

I'm not an idiot. I know what he's thinking, and I also know that he still owes me exactly seven hundred and fifty thousand parchels. Minus a bologna sandwich.

So I can piss him off, shove him away, and kiss that money goodbye. Or... I can avoid him. For at least another day.

And then it happens.

He kisses me.

His lips press fully against mine. Heavy and parting and demanding and completely suffocating. There's an anxious feeling pushing within my chest.

I shove against him hard until he stumbles back from me.

Chaos wastes no time. The dragon's storming steps bring slashing talons and sharp teeth into the Prince's face. I barely have time to throw myself between the two of them. A rumbling growl of frustration and aggression rolls off the dragon as he stalks back from me, his glaring attention held on the Prince.

"I'm so sorry. They're overly protective." I put my hand affectionately against his chest and his wild gaze finally pulls to that small touch between us. "Could we reschedule for after you've taken the little beasts off my hands." *And paid me in full.* The smile I give him is the opposite of how he's making me feel right now, but I force it to hold in place.

Let's reschedule for after I've left town. That sounds perfect. Yes, let's call it a date.

The warmth of his hand makes me tense beneath his touch as it settles low on my back.

"Of course." Once again, his gaze lowers to my lips, and despite how much I lean away from him, he pushes his lips on mine just lightly before stepping away, opening the door, and walking out of my fucking life.

For tonight at least.

A shaking breath falls from my mouth the moment he leaves. The air seems to actually reach my aching lungs now.

Chaos' strong arm slips around me, his bare chest brushing against my back. Without a word he leads me back bed. He pulls back the blankets for me. Exhaustion pulls at my body as I slip beneath the smooth quilt.

Instead of lying over me, he slips in at my side, and I don't hesitate to wrap myself around him. Corded muscle tone wraps around me as he holds me to his chest. I wish the last fifteen minutes never happened.

And that's what I pretend. I pretend Chaos fucked me sweetly, and gently, and thoroughly. And maybe slightly roughly. And now, he holds me just like this in the most caressing way I've ever felt.

I pretend it's perfect.

Until his whispered promise slips into my mind with a reminder of reality.

"If he touches you again, I'll fucking kill him."

TEN

BETWEEN A DREAM AND REALITY

A dream that's more of a memory than a dream drowns me that night. It pulls me under until I'm not sure what's real and what isn't.

It's so familiar his scent of warm cinnamon and hot embers consumes me. Glittering crimson eyes shine down on me as I recall the last time I ever saw Sinister.

"I hate myself." It's a whispered confession that sinks right through my heart. "I hate that he hurts you, and I hate that you stay." His voice is steady as it fans across my skin. He never knew that his brother literally owned my soul. "But most of all, I hate that you won't let me help you." Sinister's palm skims over the bruise along my cheek, and my insides twirl recklessly from the feel of his touch against my skin.

I was always like that. My nerves could never withstand his nearness. Until very recently, Kreedence's brother was the only man alive who ever made me feel this way. And I was too stupid to ever realize what that meant.

The sharp angles of his handsome features capture my attention as I stare up at him. His frame towers over me, but he leans into me to close the space between us.

My palm skims along the smooth inking lines twirling down his arm, and a sinking feeling in my stomach tells me he isn't real. Not even my dreams allow me to enjoy Sinster's forgotten touch. I wonder if I'll ever forget what it felt like to love him.

Even when I knew I shouldn't.

This is it. This is the moment that I ruined my life.

And his.

We were always friends. Friends with too much unspoken emotion between them. But right now, in this moment, we forgot that we were supposed to only be friends.

He's so close to me, breeding warmth and lust all through my core. He's the only person who cares about me in my life. Or at least ... he was.

I want to feel something. Past all the pain and anger, I want to feel what it'd feel like to have someone love me. If only just for a second.

My palms settle on his strong shoulders as I meld against his body for the first freeing moment in my entire life. His head lowers and he draws out every slow second of his lips brushing against mine.

It's our first and only kiss that I've relived a thousand times within my dreams. It consumes me, and it makes me ache for that feeling of lust and love that I haven't felt in five years.

Until last night.

The memory of Chaos' hands on my body flickers through my thoughts, but then Sinister's lips part mine, and I fall into the consuming feeling of his touch. Warm palms push down my spine until every inch of my body is aligned with his.

"Come with me." His lips pull away from mine before coming right back. "Come with me tonight." Another small pause for our kiss to tease one another. "Right now, Arlow." Another slow brush of his lips against mine. "You and me. Tell me you don't want that."

I kiss him harder because I can't lie. I can't tell him I don't want that. It's everything I've ever wanted, and it's everything I'll never have. Because Kreedence owns me. He owns my soul with some form of black magic that I've never even seen before. I never realized I could temporarily use a form of old magic against his until it was too late.

I never even tried until Kreedence pushed me too far. When he took Sinister, that was the breaking point. He could hurt me over and over and over again but it wasn't until he took away the one person I cared about that I fought back.

In my dream, I kiss Sinister even more, my fingers clinging to him so tightly it hurts.

Because I know.

I know it's the last time I'll ever see him alive … It's the last time I'll ever kiss someone I truly love.

And it's the last time I ever let another person care about me. My life wasn't worth the loss of his. Kreedence ripped him away from me, and I'll hate myself every day for knowing it all could have been avoided.

I wake to the sensation of his tongue flicking against the base of my neck. The salacious dream becomes a needy form of reality. His mouth against my body washes away the memory from my mind entirely. I squirm against his weight until he starts to drift lower. The rough feel of his beard teases my flesh just right. Another worshipping kiss presses to my collarbone before Chaos' hot breath fans across the top of my breasts.

Maybe I won't sell them all. Maybe I'll keep one of them for myself.

His teeth rake across my nipple from over my shirt, and I arch beneath him. My fingers fist his hair as his big palms push beneath my back to pull my aching bud fully into his mouth.

A moan shakes through me as my hips rock against his. I'm becoming entirely too attached to this one. We need space between us. Space is good.

I keep telling myself this over and over again even as I grind harder against his cock.

"Chaos—" He pushes the thin shirt away and his

tongue swirls perfectly over my sensitive skin before sucking hard. "Oh my Goddess, Chaos. Wait. Stop."

He tenses when I'm finally able to say what I know I need to say. He pulls back from me, waiting just as I instructed, but I can't seem to remember at all why I said that damn word.

"Are you okay?" His tongue rolls across his lower lip, and once again, the urge to kiss him skims through my mind.

"Yeah." My thumb brushes along the angle of his jaw. "I just have ... a lot of stuff to do today. I—I probably need to go to town to buy more food. And we need to check to see if that mage showed up—" It's not likely but I don't mention that. "And I—I just don't think we have time for sex."

Who the fuck says stuff like that? No time for sex? There's always time for sex.

Always.

But the terrifying attachment that's pulling at my little heart is a feeling so strong it overpowers my urge to see how many times he could make me orgasm.

A lot. I bet it's a lot.

Fucking emotions.

They always ruin all the good stuff.

"What if we skipped sex and I just went down on you?" It's a testing question, like he knows how much I'm struggling to say no to him. Honestly, I want to feel that beard between my thighs more than I want my next breath.

"That—that is a good alternative." I nod. He's just so damn logical. Who am I to say no to someone so smart and rational?

And...

His tongue sears lower, flicking against my navel before raking his teeth hard across my stomach.

I love the way he makes me feel. I freeze with tension steeling my spine as that foul four letter word echoes on repeat in my head.

"Mmm, no. No, I don't think there's time for that. I'm sorry."

Ugh. Let it be known, I stayed strong. Resiliently unbending.

My hands seem to have a mind of their own as I tell him no once more but push him down between my thighs.

"Low, I think maybe we should wait." A smirk tilts his lips as my thighs tighten around his hard body. "As much as I want you right now, you seem to be ... a little hesitant, and every time I fuck you, I want you relaxed. I don't want whatever thoughts are in your head right now to be a distraction." His big hands grip my thighs, and I nod to him. His palms glide against my skin. "I want you to want it."

Why does he have to sound so sexy right now?

"You're right." Continuously, and stupidly, I nod to him.

"You want to go start those errands then?"

Another jarring nod. Seconds tick by.

"You've got to let go of my hair then."

My eyes open and a wide smile graces his lips, showing me nearly all of his white teeth. Slowly, I release the tight hold I have on his soft locks.

Gently, he lowers his lips. He places a warm kiss to my stomach, his tongue sneaking out to slowly taste me. He's this sexy sweet enigma that I might never be able to understand.

The energy in my core tightens to an unbearable feeling of need.

Then he shoves off hard from the mattress before striding across the room.

And I'm left gasping for a breath to steady my pounding heart.

ELEVEN

HER HONORABLE WORD

When Chaos is fully clothed and my sex is no longer demanding his mouth, fingers, or cock, we head back to Agatha's. There's a new closeness between us as we walk. He doesn't strive to touch me or coddle me, but his arm brushes mine with nearly every step we take, and I want to lean into that small touch.

It seems to go very noticed when Kain and Rime turn our way. They've shifted back to their natural, naked form, and I guess out of some weird respect for Chaos, I don't look at their dicks.

Yes, let's all give a nice slow clap for my ability not to look at impressive dicks when shown.

I hand them their jeans and shirts, and the suspicious looks in their eyes are held on the two of us as they quickly dress.

"So," I can't seem to help the smile that is pushing

into place against my lips as I ask my innocent question, "did that mage ever turn up?"

I'm going to say no.

"No, not yet." Kain looks at me as if he doesn't trust me at all.

He's a smart man.

"Do you three intend to stay here all day waiting for her?"

"Yes," Kain says sternly.

"And then what? Will you go home? Call it quits? Maybe investigate a neighboring Kingdom for this devious but very beautiful mage?"

Did I mention beautiful?

Once more, Kain's gaze narrows a little more on me. If he keeps it up, he's just going to be squinting at me, and there's nothing intimidating about poor eyesight.

"Do you have something you want to say to me?" My chin tips up at his accusing look.

"If she's not here by this afternoon, we'll have to check in with our source for more information."

Check in. Two things cross my mind here: that gives me time to get the hell off their radar, but also …

"I'll need at least one of you to stay to make good on my deal with the Prince."

"Your deal?" Kain's head tilts at me for confirmation, and his fiery red hair catches my attention for only a second.

"Yes, I owe him three insufferably arrogant dragons. I

can make excuses for a few weeks, but he's already paid for at least one of you." My arms cross as my words come out in a steady tone. "It'd be bad for business if I didn't keep my half of the deal."

Rime's brows rise as his jaw begins to tic, and it's the only indication that he's outraged at the moment. That heavy quietness that he always has represses his angry words.

"I'm sorry; you actually think you'll be selling us to the Prince? In what fucking reality do you think that's going to happen?" Kain takes a storming step toward me.

"This one. This reality. We had a deal."

"*You* had a deal." Kain takes another single step, and his angry gaze is boring down into mine, his chest pushing against mine. The warm smell of campfire and timber wash over me in a delicious way.

"You can leave once he has you. You can eat all his fucking royal food just like you did mine, but I invested in you three. I gave my word. My word is important to me, Kain."

"I can't—I can't fucking talk to her right now." He carefully steps back from me, his jaw clenched tightly closed as he puts several feet of space between us.

Chaos comes closer to me, his shoulder warming mine as he finally stands up for me.

Finally. I hope he tells these two dragon dicks who's in the right here.

"Let's all just calm down. We'll take tonight, and we'll make a new plan tomorrow morning."

Huh. He didn't say one word about me being right.

I cock a brow at him, but he doesn't meet my waiting gaze. He avoids me entirely.

I'm not going to lie, the name Dickless is definitely circling my mind right now.

TWELVE

WHEN PASTS COLLIDE

Chaos chose them, his friends. I'm not really mad he didn't stand up for me. It was just something that made me see us in a clearer light. He and I are nothing really. The other night doesn't change our future. I need to remember that this is just business for me.

But I also can't help but like the way he still watches me even after all the space I've put between us.

In the pettiest way possible, I give a nice, long, happy stretch as I slip from my bed the following morning. The night before, I told Chaos he couldn't sleep with me. He sits in the chair opposite of my bed and watches me now with tired eyes as I push the soft sheets off my body. When I stand in only my lace panties and bra, I arch my back with my arm rising above my head, showing off every inch of sun-kissed skin as I pretend to stretch once more.

Rime and Kain sit at my kitchen table, and they

exchange a look among themselves. I pass by the poor pup near the foot of my bed, and just as I'm about to walk by without a second glance, Chaos' warm hand pushes across my hips. He pulls me back to him, forcing me to acknowledge him. I have to remember he's just another beautiful beast in my life.

You're not supposed to show weakness to a crying puppy.

And so, I don't show my emotions to Chaos.

My arms fold slowly across my chest, and his attention slips to my breasts for only a moment.

"I don't really understand any of this." His tone is quiet as he tries to make sense of what's happening here. "Are you mad at me?"

My lips part as I try to find a gentle way to tell him we're just friends. Kind of. We're *almost* just friends.

Before I can speak, Rime cuts me off.

"She's trying to tame you, Dickless." My gaze shifts to him, and I find that the two of them are finishing off the cake I bought. The bag that the bread and deli meat were brought home in just days ago lays empty and crumpled on the floor.

"Did you guys eat all of the food?"

Rime glances down at the last chunk of white cake before picking it up with his fingers and pressing it slowly into his mouth. He keeps fuck-you eye contact firmly in place the entire time.

And with all the confusing thoughts in my mind, it's just enough to make me lose it.

"Get out of my fucking house."

Rime continues his slow chewing, his legs spread wide as he gives my statement little interest.

Kain looks to his friend, his hands rising just slightly as if he might apologize.

Of course, he doesn't.

"I think you're overreacting."

"I said *get out!*" My shriek is accompanied by the smallest of thuds as my bare foot stomps against the floor.

A smile pulls at the corner of Kain's lips as his gaze dips to my breasts when they bounce slightly, and I suddenly realize I'm throwing the world's least threatening temper tantrum while standing in only my underwear.

He stands, and the two of them take their sweet time exiting. The door clicks softly closed behind them.

And there I stand, defeated and shaking with anger. But I stood my ground. I won. This is what winning feels like. I'm sure of it.

Chaos' words cut through my pathetic celebration.

"So ... you're not mad at me then?"

I give up.

I do compromise though. I think if I continue to work with Chaos, he'll be the bigger person and do what's right and let me keep my deal with the Prince. I'll just stay on his good side, and he'll stay on mine, we'll form a bond of sorts and, if I ask him nicely, he'll go with the Prince to keep my word—and, more importantly, my money. Then he can leave if he likes. He doesn't have to stay, but he does have to make it appear like I'm not a crook.

Because I'm most definitely not. I keep my word.

Until then, I need to play nice.

I lift my dress as I trail through the woods after the three men. Heat rolls through the forest, making sweat drip down my neck and back.

They're looking to meet up with their *source*. Kreedence. Fear twists through me but I smother it out with the reminder of my plans. Today will have to be a rather careful day. A plan is in place. I will just have to stick to it.

"How much farther?" It's the first time I've asked it, but it's step one in the plan.

"We're meeting him at the canyon about a mile north of here," Kain says as he pauses to look back at me.

I wipe at my brow a bit dramatically as I lean against a small oak tree. The bark bites against my skin.

If I didn't know any better, I'd think he was pitying me.

I must be a dainty looking thing right now. My hair is pulled back from my neck, my skin glistening with sweat, my long legs on display just for his viewing pleasure.

"My head is pounding, and these dizzy spells keep coming and going."

I'm a terrible person. Too many lies and bad decisions make up my life.

But it's my life. And I have to survive it.

Kain cocks a brow at me.

"Did you drink anything today?"

I've had about four glasses of water.

"A little. I was just so hungry that I didn't really think about water. I guess I haven't eaten or drank anything all day."

Because of you. Because you ate all my fucking food. Hint, hint.

Now, he does pity me. And if I'm not mistaken, there's a tiny little ounce of guilt there in his pretty eyes.

Good.

"Fuck." He trails back to me. His fingertips skim along the side of my face and his closeness makes me shift. I don't think I've been this close to him in his human form without any angry words filling the space between us. I don't think I've seen him look this caring either. "Okay. You shouldn't go any farther." Worry lines his face, and he tilts his head to the side to look over his shoulder. "Rime, stay here with her. Make sure she doesn't pass out. We'll go ahead and get the details and find her some water."

I'm much more likely to have a sensible conversation with one of them one on one. Of the three, Rime is the quietest, and I know it's not because he's shy. It's that age-old saying, if you don't have anything nice to say, don't say anything at all. Unfortunately, there's so much un-niceness within Rime, it makes him almost mute.

So, I don't know how well my little plan is going to work.

Chaos passes me a long look before trailing after his friend. I can't help but stare at his broad shoulders as he saunters off into the thick woods.

I wish our lives were different. If things were different, I'd explore the feelings that press into my chest every time I look at him.

Unfortunately, I won't be around long enough in the near future to explore anything.

The forest is very much alive today. Birds sing a crying song, like ravens giving way to warning. Leaves rustle in tune with every curious creature that runs through the long limbs that stretch high above.

"You're a good actress." Rime's words are spoken low and pointedly.

I shift on my heels, my thin dress catching on a vine of thorns for a moment.

"What makes you think I'm acting?"

He leans against a tree, his arms folded, his head tilted in a studying way as he looks at me through cruel, narrowed eyes. It's hard to believe this one was ever my favorite.

"It's easy to see. Your posture when you spoke to him changed into a defeated and helpless look that I've never seen. Your voice, which normally grates against my every nerve, was a sweet and breathy sort of sound. I actually liked that sound. You should sound like that all the time."

My jaw clenches, but I have to put real effort into forcing a friendship right now.

Even if he is a giant, insufferable dragon dick.

"What did this mage do that has you three so adamant about capturing her for your friend?"

What brought these dragons to a man like Kreedence? He stares at me for a moment longer, just long enough that I think he won't answer at all.

Until he does.

"He isn't our friend. We owe him. We're doing him this favor because we owe him. And so does the mage. This mage owes him money or an irreplaceable object of some kind. She owes him something important, and instead of delivering, she skipped town."

She owes him her soul.

The way Rime talks about me ... he hates me and he doesn't even know it. Pain stings my heart. It's not that I care. I don't know these men at all, but there's something completely awful about being hated and not having a thing you can do to change it.

I'm not an idiot. I know I'm a terrible person. I feel it deep within myself. I feel the twist of guilt every time I think about the things I've done. I just ... I think I could be different if given the opportunity. If I could just get to where I'm going. If I could get to that place of safety that's waiting for me in my future, I know I could be different.

His pretty eyes are so pale they match the morning skyline in the clearest blue I've ever seen. The sun shines against them, catching against his irises and magnifying them into a harsh color of cruelty. His glaring gaze drifts away from me, just over my shoulder, and the interest he shows makes me turn slowly.

And then I see him.

That pain in my heart pivots until it's stabbing through my stomach with sinking fear.

I've been a drifter for five years. Drifter sounds carefree, and beautiful. Even if it's not. I wasn't always a drifter. I was once a woman in love. Blinded and foolish.

I literally fell in love with a demon. It was a twisted and controlling form of love. My mother always warned me against hellacious men. She probably never thought I'd give my heart to a literal demon though.

To say I could do better is a bit of an understatement.

It's terrifying to see the man I fear standing next to the men I've started to care about.

Suddenly my past is standing right before me.

THIRTEEN

FAKING IT

Kreedence, nods as he walks side by side with Kain. The two men are opposites in every single way possible. There's a violence in the simple way Kreedence walks, like he's lashing out at the forest itself. While Kain walks with care, his steps thought out. Like he knows exactly where he's going in life. Chaos trails behind them as the two men speak. Before any of them can even spot me, my feet start off in a sprint as if the fear in me is urging me on before my mind has even thought about the magic I've saved up just for a moment like this.

At the last second, Rime grips my arm in a painful way and throws me against the tree he was just leaning against. Power stings through my fingertips. I refuse to hurt any of these men. They got caught up in the middle of something much bigger than they ever realized.

My heart is slamming and pounding against my chest, demanding fight or flight. And my magic, it's burning through my veins, preparing to use what I've hidden carefully away for too long.

Rime's gaze shifts quickly across my wide eyes. I don't know what he sees there, but it seems to turn his always aggressive features into something similar to concern. It's a softer look that makes him look younger. Sweeter.

It's like he's familiar with the fear in my features. There's this sympathy in him right now that makes me question everything I think I know about him.

He holds me firmly in place before whispering low.

"What's wrong?"

I don't look away, but I can feel Kreedence's dark energy closing in. It's this suffocating thing that snuffs out the warm summer breeze and turns it into a humidity straight from the bowels of hell.

Discreetly, I lower myself, hunching down until Rime's wide shoulders hide me completely.

"That man, he isn't who you think he is."

"And how the hell would you know, My Little Tamer?" His head tilts just slightly, but he oddly keeps his stance, hiding me entirely.

I don't know why he isn't tossing me at the feet of the demon. It's confusing, but I find myself suddenly liking Rime for the first time since the three men were revealed to me.

I have to have an excuse though. If I confess I'm a mage who very much does owe that demon something, then he'll shove me into the danger I've avoided for five years.

I need a lie.

"He's a demon, Rime. I've seen him in my dreams." That's not really a lie. My nightmares are more like it. His eyes flash with interest. "If he finds me, he'll kill me. I just know it." Also not a lie. Look at me being the epitome of honesty right now.

Twigs snap and I know he's closer. Probably only a few yards separate me from the hell I once knew so well.

"Please?" The shaking way that words slips from my lips has his strong hands caressing me instead of gripping me. My whispered plea makes his eyes flare with a bright color. It's like watching the ice thaw on the coldest day of winter. The pale color turns to a deep blue and my lips part from the sight of it.

In an instant, his big palm leaves my arm and grips firmly beneath my thigh. He brings it up high until I'm locked around his lean hip, my core aligned in a sensual way with his hips.

"I'm just going to assume you're spectacular at giving a fake orgasm. You look like the type."

His words make my brows pull together with confusion, but he doesn't give me time to feel insulted. Hard and grinding thrusts have his hips pushing just perfectly against my clit.

My breath catches and I still don't know what he's doing.

"Rime, what the fuck are you doing?" Kain's outrage

makes me tense even as energy coils tightly within my core. "Fuck, I'm sorry, Kreedence." Kain's apology is quieter but it doesn't mask his annoyance.

I can't tell how close they are to us, but Rime dips his head lower to mine. His temple rests against mine, his breath fanning against my lips as his hard cock rocks against my clit once more.

"That's your cue, My Little Faker."

I pause for less than half of a second before a loud and shaking moan is forced out of me. I give a breathy little sigh at the end that makes him smirk.

My head tips back against the rough bark at the sight of his smile, his hips still rocking firmly against mine. He's really sexy when he smiles. His sharp features are normally so cruel and calculating. But when he smiles, pure sinful sexuality.

"That was the worst fake orgasm I've ever heard." The teasing sound of his voice almost deters the building tension within my sex.

My palms push against his chest before my fingers sink into his corded biceps. Just slightly, I shift my hips, meeting his thrusts enough to make my lashes flutter. His jaw tightens as a low groan shakes from his lips.

"Maybe you should be worried about why you have such extensive knowledge of what a fake orgasm sounds like."

Once more, he gives a smile like alluring danger and desire.

In this moment ... I don't completely hate him.

His head tilts until his lips skim against the curve of my neck. Hot flicks of his tongue have my breath shaking, and I have to force myself to keep my eyes open. I don't know why he's going the extra mile in this performance, why he's kissing the sensitive spot at the base of my neck but he's helping me, and I can't bring myself to question it. I lean up until I can see over his shoulder.

Only tangled vines and wide tree trunks surround us. The smattering shades of green leaves are all that can be seen.

Kreedence is gone.

The fear—that I had nearly forgotten about thanks to Rime—leaves me entirely.

"They're gone." My fingers skim up his throat, my palm settling against his sharp jawline as his pulse pounds against my touch. "Rime, it's okay, they're gone." My lashes flutter once more as he grinds himself hard against my clit.

A real moan hums over my lips, and he pulls back just slightly to meet my gaze. His breaths come in rapid heaps, and I can't help but hope he won't stop.

The curious attention in his gaze dips low until he's studying my lips. Static energy sparks between us for several seconds. It's like nothing I've ever felt. It's an energy that tingles between him and I and it's all I can think about.

Until he pushes off abruptly from the tree.

I swallow hard as my thighs rub together, already missing his strong body against mine.

"For the record, I've never been good at faking it."

"Mmm, but you have faked it."

I take a deliberate step closer to him and, just to piss him off, I smooth the wrinkles from his cotton shirt, just around his strong arms. I fuss about it for a few seconds.

"Some men," I meet his eyes with my own look of cruel amusement, "are impossible to tame in any situation."

His eyes narrow on me before he steps away from me once more.

"Consider that the last favor I do for you. There's very little kindness within me. Don't expect it from us. Dragons are not pretty pets. And we are not ones to be *tamed*."

My arms fold across my chest, and just to push him a little harder, I decide to ask what I intended to ask Chaos.

"Actually, there is another favor I need to ask."

His head turns quickly to pin me with an astounded stare. The iciness of his eyes has returned. They're no longer a deep blue but the coldest frost I've ever seen.

"You seriously have the balls to ask me for a favor after I just gave you the best fake orgasm you've ever had?" He doesn't smile as he says it, but I can't help but smirk at his words. A warm feeling spreads all through me. Even his sarcasm is ... different. Less teasing and too serious for me to really get a feel for how he's feeling.

He's not going to be joking when I ask him what I need to ask him.

"Next week, I need one of you to let me take you to

the Prince. He's given me half down. I'm willing to walk away from the other half, and you'll never have to deal with me again. You can even have my shack while you look for your astoundingly beautiful mage."

"Fine." His arms cross, mirroring my stance even as surprise strikes through me at how easily he just gave in. "But we'll go tonight. I don't intend to waste a week with you, My Little Tamer. The faster you're out of my life, the better."

My stomach knots around itself as I realize he not only hates the mage he's been told about, but he also hates me. There's no misleading reasons for why he dislikes me.

He hates me for me.

FOURTEEN

AS WHITE AS SNOW

Kain doesn't mention it. If he's frustrated with the fake fuck fest his friend put on while he was working, he never mentions it.

He does pass me long and questioning glances throughout the day. He's giving me one right now as I cup my hands within the cool river before bringing the water to my lips. He watches every single move I make down to the way the water drips from my lips and down my throat.

"Kreedence talked almost fondly about the mage today." A teasing smirk touches the corner of Chaos' full lips.

Rime brings his attention to Chaos. Chaos stands back, seemingly ready to head home as he lingers near the woods while Rime leans against a tree, one ankle crossed lazily over the other.

It's even weirder that Chaos doesn't mention what

happened either. It's as if he didn't just see his friend supposedly fucking me in front of him ...

Guilt twists through me and I can't stop watching him. I hate my feelings. I hate the mess I've made of my life.

But most of all, I hate the position I just put Chaos in with his friend.

Kain and I sit in the damp grass near the river's edge. The smell of pine is heavy in the fresh air, and I breathe it in deeply on a shaking breath. The water is barely a trickle here; a calming sound that fills the quiet forest while these two discuss my ex right in front of me, and I pretend not to listen at all.

Rime doesn't reply to that statement, but he does consider it. He seems to pick apart what people say and now is no different.

"I wonder what the woman did to him. Seems he was stupid enough to fall in love with her." Kain's emerald eyes skim to the tangle of thick tree limbs above, letting the pieces of sunlight warm his skin.

"You sound so jaded." I bite my lip the moment I say it. Sometimes the words just slip out. I'll blame it on my normal lack of a social life. I was supposed to be minding my own business.

The look Kain shoots me says he thinks I should mind my own business as well. Chaos' dark brow arches at me, almost sending me a warning signal with a single look.

"I'm not jaded. I'm *careful*. Responsibility makes

someone careful. I don't back down from commitments or responsibility. You just have to be careful in life."

Hmm, sounds jaded. And no one knows jaded better than I do.

"Who was the woman who made you so careful?" Once again, I lecture myself about minding my own business, and, once again, I ignore that little chastising voice.

Kain doesn't look angry this time. His attention holds on me, shifting over my features slowly. For a moment, I think he'll actually tell me. Then his gaze tears from mine.

"We need to get back." He stands, leaving me behind as he starts walking back into the thicket of the woods.

Chaos shakes his head before trailing after his friend in a rush like he might comfort him.

Rime watches him go as he passes by, his arms folded neatly in place before he shoves away from his spot against the tree. Thin twigs snap under his boots, and he startles me when he pauses at my side. We stare at one another in an awkward beat of silence. Stiffly, he lowers his hand to me, and it takes me a moment to realize I should take this small offer of kindness from him. His warm palm grips mine, pulling me to my feet until we're chest to chest. The clear blue of his eyes studies my features as I tip my head up to him. The feel of his breath against my lips is a cold and tingling feeling. He searches every part of my eyes, looking for something there. Or ... maybe he's trying to understand me.

When his animalistic gaze makes something in my

core tighten, I pull away, letting my palm fall to my side finally. That sparking energy seems to swirl within the small space between us, skimming over my flesh in waves.

"You two coming?" Kain's voice yells out to us, and it seems to break the building tension immediately.

My gaze flickers to Rime's once more before I turn away, trailing after the sound of his friend's voice.

And forgetting all of those confusing emotions the moment he's out of sight.

Kain sits on my kitchen table, his long legs nearly touching the floor as he lazily discusses the details with Chaos and Rime.

And I'm left forgotten as I listen intently. I'm all but taking notes about what they're saying, and no one seems to think to filter themselves in front of me.

"Kreedence is adamant that she's in this area. He says the mage was chased out of the town east of here for accidentally setting fire to a crop field when they tried to burn her at the stake. The people were pissed she wouldn't just accept her punishment." Kain almost smirks, and his eyes lock with mine as I smile a cocky reminiscing smile.

As if I'd really just let them burn me at the stake.

How insulting.

I didn't intend to burn everything in a ten mile radius but... incidents happen.

"So, she's dangerous?" Rime's long fingers tap against the tabletop. He sits lazily in the chair, his legs spread out wide and invitingly.

Laughter shakes through Chaos and soon Kain is laughing right along with him.

"Hardly. Kreedence said the most dangerous thing about her is her mouth that never shuts up." Kain's smirk irks me to my core.

My lips part with outrage, but I manage to snap my mouth closed before the protests leave me.

"Rime," I call out, standing abruptly. I don't have to sit here and listen to my shitty ex-boyfriend fill my friends' heads with lies … not that they're my friends …

Rime's smile falters as his attention settles on me.

"You did say today, didn't you?"

I don't give further details into what he's volunteered to do. Our agreement is between us and us alone.

"Speaking of mouths that never shut up." He doesn't deter his gaze as he speaks, and it makes me want to climb up the table and wrap my hands around his neck.

The anger in me rises and, before I can stop it, the fuming words are spewing out of me.

"Listen, dragon dick, I might talk a lot, but at least I'm not blindly following orders from a man who's literally sent from hell. Maybe you should reevaluate your life choices, asshole." My steps shake across the old floorboards, and I slam the door behind me as I storm outside.

Grim gives a low whine of concern, his bushy tail held low while he makes his way toward me. The warmth of his blazing body leans into me, and my palm pushes across his fuming fur.

I wish all the creatures in my life were as sweet and caring as Grim. He's been the only creature I've ever kept. Partly because I love him, and partly because no one seems to want to buy a fiery hellhound who may or may not be cursed. He's one of a kind. Because the rest of his kind are in hell.

"It's their loss, isn't it, Grim.?" I tilt my head against his, and the heat of his tongue sears across my cheek as he gives me a happy kiss.

If only all my creatures were as loving.

"What happened with you and Rime in the woods?" Chaos's voice startles me, and he doesn't look at me as I stare up at him. "I don't—I don't believe you two were actually fucking—"

"You don't?" I cut off his steady stream of words. Was my fake orgasm really that bad? I don't know why I want to take such pride in a fake orgasm, but it does kind of sting my ego to think he knows I was faking.

"For one, I couldn't smell your arousal like I could the other night."

My brows arch at him, my lips parting without any words aiding me whatsoever.

"I'm sorry, what?" I finally sputter.

"I could smell it, sure, but it wasn't that delicious flooding scent." He pushes his hands into his pockets as a strange smile starts to pull at his lips. "So, whatever it was that you two were doing, it wasn't fucking. And also, even if you were, it doesn't bother me the way you think."

I stand and his fingers brush along the back of my knuckles before he slips his hand into mine. His strong body is solid against my arm as he stares into my eyes.

"I saw the pitying look you were giving me. Dragons are different. Sharing a mate—I mean someone I care about with someone who I also care about—strengthens our bond. It makes a feeling of pride burn through me, not jealousy. I just, I didn't want you to feel awkward around Rime and me."

My heart is warm and pounding as he leans closer to me. My gaze catches his every miniscule movement as he closes the space between his lips and mine. Ache blooms through me as I tip my head up to him.

The door bangs shut, and I jump at the sound of it.

"Let's get this date over with, My Tamer." Rime strides down the road as if he's going to the Prince with or without me.

I pass a knowing and annoyed look to Grim before glancing back at Chaos. The hellhound's crimson gaze follows the arrogant man as a low, humming growl emits from his throat.

"I feel the same way." A huffing sigh shoves from my lungs, but then Chaos presses his lips to the side of my temple.

His warm attention lingers on me before he walks backward a few steps, turns and strides into the house without another word. I stare after him for several seconds before I realize Rime is practically out of sight already.

I have to nearly jog after Rime. Dirt billows around my bare feet, and he doesn't even seem to notice me when I finally reach his side. The way they mocked me for my apparently incessant talking presses to the front of my mind, and I force myself not to say anything to him.

I try my very best to keep my mouth shut. I don't talk an obscene amount. It's just that I never have anyone to talk to. Goddess forbid I make conversation from time to time with the asshole dragons who I've kindly taken into my home and fed and watered every day. "Is it too much to ask that they pretend to show me kindness?"

"Yes."

I pause my little rant and glare up at him from the corner of my eye.

I didn't realize I'd said anything aloud, but now that I have, I'm going to be silent for the remainder of our little trip.

Total silence.

We will see how he likes being ignored.

I refuse to say a word.

"You know you can't just waltz into the Kingdom in your human form?" My tone is an angry and annoyed sound that even I shake my head at.

I was doing so well with my vow of silence too.

But seriously, I can't offer the Prince a man full of hostility in place of a mystical and beautiful dragon.

That's not a good trade at all. No one wants a man when they could have a dragon instead.

I'll take my white dragon over a white knight any day.

... That sounds a little disgustingly romantic. That's not what I meant at all.

The quietness is pushing into my chest in the form of anxiety with each passing second.

"You can't walk in there as a man, Rime." The words shriek from my lips, and the tone of my anger has him halting in an instant.

He stares down at me, his jaw ticking just slightly. He's intimidating, I'll admit it. But something about him doesn't scare me. I know what a cruel man looks like, and the hard features of the man before me aren't it. He's just used to being closed off I think. I can't imagine how shut off he felt growing up without much human contact.

He helped me. He pushed aside his cold demeanor long enough to help me. I don't believe there's really a malicious bone in his body.

While his gaze is locked with mine, shimmering scales begin creeping across his jaw line. They look snow kissed, and it takes me a moment to realize what's happening.

His palm connects with my shoulder. More glittering scales begin ripping through his flesh and that sexy smile pulls across his lips just as he shoves me hard away from him.

My ass hits the ground, my palms stinging against the

earth as I watch, in awe of the man before me who transforms with swirling magic into a massive, roaring dragon.

A shadow falls over me as his wings spread wide and he takes flight. A cold chill hits the air, and I barely have time to raise my hand as a heavy frost rains down from the dragon's mouth. The ice clatters to the ground, breaking like glass around me but not on me. Fine particles of snow glisten against my long hair, blanketing my skirt, and I tip my head up to meet the flakes. Several land against my lips, and I breathe them in like it's the first breath of air I've ever experienced. In a way, it is. It's the first time I've ever felt snow. The winter temperature here never lowers long enough for the frost to settle in.

In my entire life, I've never realized I wanted something that I've never even had.

His long wings soar for a moment before he glides lower. With grace and beauty, he lands before me, his head held obnoxiously high.

The small and helpless dragon I found weeks ago no longer exists. He's the largest beast I've ever seen. Muscle lines his arms. His solid frame, and even his tail, is a weapon to be feared.

He's in his dragon form, but he's still not the favorite, quiet little creature I loved. He stares down at me with impatience, and it takes me a moment to stand, dusting my skirt off as I try to find my confidence again in front of this mountain of an animal.

His wing lowers to me, and I stare at that offering for a moment. It's held out purposefully to me, bending against the ground at my feet. Hesitantly, I place my foot against his smooth scales. Wings are fragile, made up of delicate bones and thin structure. But he doesn't seem to flinch away from me as I brace my foot against his upper wing. I reach for something, anything to grab onto.

There's nothing. Only smooth scales and hard muscle.

Without warning, his cold snout brushes against the curve of my ass and he pushes. I bite back my shriek of fear as he helps me up. My hair is across my face, stuck to my lips, and a mess of dark locks blocks my sight when I finally settle in against his spine. I barely have time to push my hair back before his wings are beating down on the dusty earth. I meld my body against his, wishing I had something to hold on to.

Would he let me fall?

If I fell, there'd be no more secrets between us. He'd definitely see my magic come out during a life or death situation.

Another sheet of ice and snow rips through him, and the tension in my shoulders leaves me as the flakes begin to flurry around me. I lift myself just slightly to see the world below us pass by in colors of late summer. The leaves are tinged with amber colors like autumn is just seconds away from turning the world around me into crisp beauty. Another shaking roar rumbles within him and he rains down more of the pretty flakes and glittering ice. The wide fields below are a blanket of white glistening in the warm sunlight.

It'll all be gone in a matter of minutes.

But it's here now.

I raise my hand to the cold winds and let the damp flakes kiss my skin, sending a shiver all through me. Rime peers back at me from the corner of his icy eye, and I lift both hands letting my legs lock firmly around him. He pauses for only a second before an earth-shaking roar tears through him with another bout of ice and snow. My chin tips up to the feel of it against my skin and I let out an excited yell to match his roar.

For only a moment, I feel alive and wild.

For only a moment, I'm every bit the free-spirited drifter I've appeared to be for the last five years.

All because of Rime.

FIFTEEN

THE FAVORITE

The guards at the palace aren't nearly as happy about Rime's winter wonderland. The dragon soars high above the castle gates, even going as far as to kick off the top of the bricks that read *Blessed Minden, Saved by the Solstice Queen*, letting the wall crumble beneath his touch as he settles down on the ground in front of the castle doors. His destruction tumbles, landing hard at his side, but he doesn't give the heaping mess a second glance.

The showoff.

All the king's horses and all the king's men show up at once. Huh, so that's what it takes to get some service around here.

All I got last time was John. And he wasn't very welcoming at all.

I leap down from the dragon, impressing even myself when I don't stumble against the dirt. I raise my chin high with my loyal dragon at my side. Or at least ... he appears loyal. For the moment.

Gleaming swords are directed our way, the guard's unwavering and fierce attention not held on me but the silent dragon.

Rime gives them a careless look as if he doesn't care to acknowledge their expensive weapons and shining armor.

"Good morning to you too." My chipper voice is hardly noticed. "Excuse me, where's John this afternoon? John?" I call out to him. It takes a few seconds before my favorite guard pushes through the iron-clad men.

"John, how are you?" His sword lowers, and he passes a sheepish look to his friends.

"I'm going to need you to start making appointments. Your entrances are becoming more and more dramatic every time I see you."

A pleased smile tilts my lips.

"John, I have a special delivery for Prince Linden." I give a wave of my hand to the beast at my side.

John's attention skims up the massive frame of Rime, and his eyes widen as he takes in the creature before he finally nods and turns toward the castle.

John does know how to get things done around here. I hope the King promotes him for his quick service.

"I will announce your arrival." He stalks away, but I do hear the mumbled words he speaks next. "Though I'm sure he's already well aware."

Minutes drift by and I pass the time by taunting the

men. My fingertip taps against the tip of the blade poised at my face. I flick it a few times and the man's eyes narrow on me.

These men are well acquainted with me. They've had to suffer through my antics about once a month for over a year now.

Ah, the poor bastards. I wonder what they do when I'm not around. It must be a boring day when I don't grace them with my lovely presence.

John's gait is slower now as he comes back to my side.

"He said..." John pauses as if it pains him to say what he's about to say. "He said he'd like you and your beast to come inside."

I tilt my head.

"Did you tell him my pet has grown a little since he saw him last?"

John nods apologetically. The men slowly lower their swords, but they keep a close eye on us as I hesitantly walk toward the front doors. It's a wide entrance. Two doors are opened at the center for us by two pretty women who watch Rime with wide and fearful gazes.

"Be-have," I say to the dragon through clenched teeth.

I pretend not to worry if my sweet little pet will take out the front door with his long white horns. Or if he'll open his wings at just the right moment and wipe out the castle walls entirely. I act like he is the perfectly tamed beast that I say he is.

An open room with only a table at the center is

before us. The glossy white tiles lead to a curving staircase on the left that disappears into the second floor. It's all very shining, beautiful and, of course, expensive. The gleaming chandelier at the center of the large room is like money itself hanging from the ceiling. It's all gold detail and too many parchels wasted just to demand attention from its viewers.

The doors close with a loud thump, and only when we're secluded and alone do I turn to him. I double-check the massive wooden doors, my gaze flickering over every brick to make sure all is as it should be.

The dragon's wings are tucked in tightly and he waits with stiff posture, his gaze peering down at me momentarily.

Hmm, he's being oddly obedient.

Maybe I have tamed him well after all.

From behind me, footsteps sound high above on the stairs, somewhere on the second floor it sounds like.

Rime's either trying to get back on my good side or—

Right before my eyes the large dragon begins to swirl in a cloud of pale smoke. My lips part with terror.

Please no.

I check over my shoulder. No one's here.

But those footsteps are growing closer by the second.

When I turn back around, there before me, in all his fucking beautiful nakedness, is Rime. A cruel smile pulls at his full lips as he tilts his head at me to glare down on me from beneath his thick lashes.

Fuck, fuck, fuck.

"Change back." I point aimlessly at the ground, my foot stomping against the smooth white tile.

"No." His arms fold across his chiseled chest. "I think I look better like this, don't you agree?" He lifts his arms as if to show me the full package.

As if I haven't seen his full fucking package a dozen times now.

"You're going to get us killed. Change back."

"You're not a very nice person, Arlow. Neither am I." His speech spikes fear into me with every second that passes. "Do you think your perfect Prince would be angry to find you with a naked man instead of the fierce dragon you promised him?"

The footsteps become louder and, when I realize the asshole isn't going to be the good fucking pet that I pretend he is, I grip his arm. In a rush, I shove him into the closest closet.

I could use my magic to lock him in there. I could silence him with a wave of my hand. And explain this all to Linden with the most logical of excuses.

Until Rime grips my wrist and pulls me into the closet with him.

I peer out at the Prince's shining shoes that I can barely see coming down the curving staircase. With my heart pounding, I do the only thing I can think of: I close the door.

Darkness secludes us, but it doesn't seem to change the fact that I know he's smirking. My arms fold across my chest as I listen intently.

"We should probably be quiet," he stage whispers just as the steps outside come to a halt.

"Please do not say a word," I say under my breath.

A dominant step brings his body flush against mine. His chest presses against my breasts, and I tip my head up at him to see the shadows of his sharp features.

"I won't say a word."

The warmth of his body seeps into mine, attempting to distract me with his nearness.

His head tilts and I tense in confusion as his lips brush the side of my neck. A shaking breath claims my lungs. I snap my mouth closed as his tongue sears over my throat before he presses another slow kiss to my collarbone. I feel that kiss in a much deeper place but the confusing way my body reacts to his annoys me as well as intrigues me.

I know this is a testing and tormenting game he's playing. But all I can think about is how good his hands feel locked around my hips even as the Prince's voice cuts through the darkness.

Rime's distracting; too distracting, and too good with his mouth. I think he's right; we're both terrible people who keep throwing each other into terrible situations. His nipping teeth against my neck feels like a test to see if I'll out myself rather than allowing him to do it. I'm not going to. I still have a chance at the money that will build my future. And I refuse to let Rime ruin that for me because his tongue is more talented than I ever realized.

"Where is she?" the Prince asks.

Big palms push against my breasts from over my shirt, his thumbs rubbing slow circles over my nipples.

"Don't make a sound, My Tamer. Wouldn't want your Prince to catch you being mauled by a dragon." Warm hands push down the collar of my shirt until his rough palm brushes against my breast.

Mauled by a Dragon. I nearly roll my eyes but, instead, my eyes roll back in my head as his mouth covers my nipple entirely. A hushed gasp parts my lips as my head tips back against the wall.

He thinks he's so fucking smart.

This was a set up all along. He had no intention of going with the Prince.

My fingers push against his hair, holding his head in place as he sucks hard before rolling his tongue against my sensitive skin.

A shaking moan hums through me, and it's then that I make a choice.

Like I said, I only use my magic in life or death situations. This feels like one of those times, I think.

With a wave of my hand, dark smoke eases from my palms. It's unseen among the shadows, but I feel it as it veils us.

Rime doesn't seem to see it. And I'm not going to make him aware of it.

I'm not going to distract him. Who am I to interrupt him when he's showing his talents?

"You taste so fucking good." The rasping sincerity in

his voice hums along my skin, making me shift against him.

My skirt brushes against my thighs as he lowers himself. His soft lips press to my abdomen. His teeth rake sharply against my lower stomach as he pushes my thin skirt and underwear down. When the skirt pools at the floor, he takes my thigh and pushes it up until my foot is propped against his smooth shoulder.

The pounding of my heart is all I hear until the Prince's voice distracts me for only a moment.

"Just go look for her. I'll wait here."

"Fuck," I whisper.

A humming laugh shakes through Rime

I almost say the angry thoughts that are flooding my mind. Until a cold breath fans against my inner thigh. Tingles rush all through me. Rough palms grip my hips as his lips skim ever so lightly against my skin just above where I want him most. Another cool breath sends a shiver across my flesh before a heated and searing breath consumes my sex. He's toying with me, and it's making me crazy.

I'm nearly shaking and he hasn't even touched me yet.

His mouth presses against my sex, and he licks me hard, spreading me with his tongue, swirling against my clit until I cry out just like he wants.

My magic holds on to every sound I make, holding it close for only us to hear. It intensifies every shaking breath I take, and the sounds of my pleasure only seem to fuel him on.

He groans against me, and the feel of it shakes into me, making my legs weak. Palms push against my ass, and he holds me to his mouth as he devours me so deeply I can't seem to catch my breath. His mouth fucks me in a carnally rough way. His tongue rolls against my folds before he sucks hard, his teeth scraping just enough to make my sex clench forcefully with the intensity of my orgasm. The moment I come, the moment my sex starts to clench around nothing, he sucks harder. His tongue seems to move quicker now, tasting every part of my orgasm until I can't even think straight.

His name is like a curse on my lips as I rock my hips against his mouth once more before relaxing into the feel of the release.

"So fucking good." One more chaste kiss slides against my sex and I can't decide if it feels romantic or animalistic.

He finally lowers his hands from my body, and I feel the space between us like it's more distance than I've ever seen.

My breath comes in heaps as I wait for my heartbeat to settle within my chest. That sparking energy is alive between us, making me feel more connected to him than I am with even myself.

I suppose I was wrong about Rime knowing a little too much about what a fake orgasm sounds like ...

The sound of my heavy breaths is all there is until the Prince speaks once more.

"You're sure it was her?"

"Is there another woman walking around the Kingdom with an forty-foot dragon, my lord?"

Ouch. John needs to watch his tone.

Seconds tick by before logic seems to settle in.

"He ... didn't hear you?" Rime's voice is nothing short of amazed.

"Well, it wasn't *that* good, to be honest." The lie is spoken casually even when my weak knees nearly give out as I bend to pull up my skirt.

His breath is against my cheek when I stand, his body heat washing into me.

"Yeah, I know you're ridiculously hard to please, but your pussy isn't. I know what it feels like, sounds like, and tastes like when a woman comes on my mouth."

My breath catches, unable to even think after the words he just spoke. Before my poor little mind has a chance to even think of a reply, the door swings open and Rime stalks out, his firm ass basking in the sunlight as he strides right up to the Prince.

The arrogant dragon dick is in for a rude awakening.

The Prince's gaze turns toward the open closet, looking right at me but not seeing me from beneath my magic. Quietly, I sneak out. Rime is still staring eye to eye with the Prince.

I bet the beautiful dragon has never felt overlooked in his entire gorgeous life.

He's about to find out what that feels like.

John is just walking through the open door as I wander outside.

Rime turns his head one way and then the other as the Prince stares through him. I have no more hiding left. He'll realize it soon enough.

This is my goodbye.

This is how my story ends with these dragons. And what a sendoff he gave me. Well done. He is my favorite after all.

A scowl tilts his lips, and it's like I can literally see everything in his little, slow-turning mind.

The way his jaw tics holds my attention for a moment before I finally meet his eyes. I stand in the warm sunlight just outside the castle doors. He stands in the center of the room, sending glaring hate toward me from several yards away.

"You're the fucking mage?"

A gnawing sort of guilt sinks through my stomach even as I push a smile in place against my lips. I force the magic within me, demanding that it surface. I need it now more than ever. I hold my middle finger up, and my lips press together as I blow him a mocking kiss.

Just before inky smoke wafts around me, pulling me away from the mess I've made in an instant.

SIXTEEN

THE MAGE

When I land in my shack, I start dumping money into my satchel. The thing looks empty and small, but the inside of it expands with magic with every fistful of money that I toss into it. I sit on my knees attempting to put every parchel I have inside. Money slips from my fingers and I scramble after it. My knee slices against a rusting nail as I trail after the mess of money.

Kain and Chaos stand around me passing each other confused glares as I race through the house like a madwoman.

His roar is heard before he's seen. The sound of it chills the air. My heart sinks as I realize how many thousands of parchels I'll have to leave behind.

His bare feet are storming across the room, and I have to physically race away from him to try to get to my bag.

It topples over before I can reach it, spilling out crisp money against the wooden floor.

"Rime, what are you doing?" Kain takes a single step between me and the deadly man ahead of me.

Rime looks from me to the bag I keep staring at.

"This is what you want, right? Money is the whole fucking thing that probably got you into this mess. You're so fucking pretty but your selfishness is ugly, Arlow." Rage stings his every word, and when he grips the bag and holds it high and taunting above me, I lunge at him, pushing past Kain to try to reach the only thing that's keeping me here.

He has no idea how deep my selfishness really is. I'll choose myself again and again and again if it means we'll live through this all. Because I've already lost one person I cared about. I can't let anyone else near enough to allow that to happen again. Selfishness is the only thing I have to keep the people around me safe.

Selfishness is so similar to loneliness sometimes.

"She's the fucking mage." Rime's eyes are frost-kissed and filled with hostility.

The moment his words settle, everyone's attention is on me.

Kain's big hand grips ahold of my wrist in an almost painful way.

My jaw clenches. Slowly my gaze meets Chaos' pretty eyes. Confusion and hurt shine there and it's hard for me to admit that I hurt him.

I hate that I hurt him above all else.

He's too sweet to hurt even if that wasn't my intention. I never meant to hurt them, I just meant ... to survive long enough to find the future I want so badly.

I swallow hard and with more force than I knew I was capable of, my magic rips through me and is fuming around them, pinning them in their place. My lips purse together as I pull my arm away from Kain. His eyes shift even as I hold his big body in the hands of my powerful magic. It's exhausting. The power within me is crying for rest, but I have to keep pushing.

My heartbeat is drilling through my chest, my eyes held wide on the man before me.

"I'm sorry I lied." *Fuck, I'm sorry.* "But I'm not some manipulating sorceress." My tone dips and still I hold his gaze. "I'm just a woman who was stupid enough to fall in love." The words fall out of my mouth, and I can't seem to stop them. "I don't owe Kreedence money." My voice quiets with rampant emotion. "I promised him my heart. I was too naive to realize he wanted my soul."

Just as my eyes close, my chest shaking for a breath, the walls around me burst.

It takes only a moment for me to realize I'd released my hold on them. Three massive and roaring dragons take form before me. Their wings spread wide until they break through the thin walls of the place I've called home for over a year. My attention flickers to the helpless fish near my bed and he watches the scene before him with big, pressured eyes. But he's safe. For now.

With a fiery breath, Kain torches the bag on the floor.

Money bursts out from the magically enclosed satchel. Parchels waft through the air, singed and burning, causing ash to drift about.

"Stop. Stop!" It burns my palms, but the paper is nothing more than crisps of ash when they hit my skin. I sink to my knees staring around at the destruction of my home.

All my hard work lies in ashes, and there's nothing I can do about it.

All of this was for nothing.

A growling bark is so loud it drowns out their roars, and Grim is by my side in an instant. His soft fur is hot against my skin as his hulking frame shields me from the reckless dragons.

In a way, I know I did this to myself. I was so set on starting a new life I couldn't see what I was doing to myself.

I put myself in danger.

Again.

My palm pushes aimlessly through Grim's thick hair, and he settles against my touch. I pull him hard against me and bury my face into his soft fur.

Moments pass, and the steady sound of their footsteps is the only sign that I'm no longer surrounded by the creatures but the men.

I don't know if there's much of a difference anymore.

Both are just as deadly.

"How do I know you're not lying?" Kain's voice is

commanding, but I don't have the energy to look at him. Or even answer him.

Fuck him. If he doesn't believe me, then fuck him.

"Kreedence isn't exactly too trusting. He's a demon," Chaos says.

"And she's a lying mage. She led us around here by our dicks. Helping us look for the mage when she was the damn mage the entire time." Kain isn't forgiving, and I don't ask him to be. I have nothing to apologize for.

"She was afraid. She never said she wasn't the mage."

I can almost feel the glare Kain is giving Chaos right now. I embarrassed them. I put them in danger.

A beat passes while they seem to consider me.

All I wanted was a life. A real life. Not a life of hiding; terrified that the man I promised my heart to would come to reap my soul.

He seemed so genuine. I actually thought he loved me.

I'll never be stupid enough to make that mistake again.

And I guess I might not even get the chance to.

"I think she's telling the truth." Rime's statement makes me tense with uncertainty.

I lift my head from Grim to stare up at his frost colored eyes. Anger seems to be tightly coiled up within him. He's a man of too much pent-up aggression and it shows. But there's a softness in his glittering eyes.

Just like when I was honest with him in the woods, he believes me. My quiet honesty seems to sink right into him and tears away at the walls he holds so close around his emotions.

Maybe he doesn't hate me after all.

"If she owed him money, she could have easily repaid it today. Kreedence is a demon. There's nothing more valuable to him than power and life itself. He feeds off it."

A chill scurries down my spine, but I don't show it. I keep my jaw locked in place.

I feel like I can almost breathe again. Rime trusts me. He believes me.

"We owe him the mage." Kain's cruel words suck the happiness right out of me. He's too logical to let his emotions pity me for even a moment.

Rime lowers himself, crouching down until we're eye level. He studies me intently as if he can see all my sins just with one dark look.

"Well, he's not getting this one."

SEVENTEEN

HIS FILTHY MOUTH

"I hope you're prepared to fight for your life." Kain crosses his arms over the hard panes of his chest, pulling my attention to his body for only a moment. "We need to leave before dusk."

"Probably would have helped if we had money." I bite the words out before I can stop them.

Rime cocks a brow at me and my smart mouth.

"The Prince will be checking on me after what happened today." I cock a brow right back at him.

And then we're both smiling.

Why am I such an idiot?

"Let's go to Agatha's for now. I'll get supplies there."

"Supplies. Like abnormal witchy supplies for your witch magic?" Kain's tone is cold and angry and, when I stand, my shirt skimming against the smooth panes of his chest, he doesn't flinch away.

"No, like normal average supplies and average clothes

for your average cock." A cough that sounds slightly like a laugh shakes through Chaos. "I can't go back to town to get you clothes, and I'm not starting a life of hiding with three naked men."

His glare narrows on me before he finally speaks.

"Average is an understatement."

That's what he takes away from my words.

Really?

Kain turns away, his steps crunching over the old boards of my home as he heads toward the road. Chaos passes me a quiet glance, his fingers skimming against mine before he trails after his friend.

Then it's just Rime and me.

A warm feeling spreads through me as I realize he's the only reason I'm not in Kreedence's possession right now.

Chaos would have stood up for me. I know he would have. But his vote would have been out numbered.

"I could leave. I could run away, and you three could say you never found me." He stands only a few feet from me and that space gets smaller and smaller with every slow step he takes.

They could be rid of me so easily. I'm more work than I'm worth, I promise. I'm a total fuck up from start to finish.

I'm a liar. A desperate, compulsive, terrible woman.

But I can't seem to say that to him.

Even if I think he already knows.

His palm skims against the curve of my neck before

trailing against my throat to push through my hair. Pain stings lightly along my scalp as his fingers fist into my locks, tilting my head up a little more to meet his intense gaze.

"I know what it's like to travel alone. I did that for a long time before I met Kain and Chaos." His gaze becomes that warm blue color, and it makes me lean into his hard body. "I know you're capable of doing all of this on your own." There's still a hard undertone to his voice that doesn't reflect the sweet way he's looking at me. His head tilts just slightly before his whispered words skim across my lips. "I'm telling you that you don't have to."

His lips nearly press to mine. My lashes nearly flutter closed. My wall that I've worked so hard to build up nearly comes toppling down.

All because this man with pretty eyes said a few pretty words to me.

I pull back from him with my breath caught in my lungs. My gaze darts to the floor as I avoid the look in his eyes.

An irrational fear claws through me, telling me that if I let myself care too much for him, for any of them, that I'll lose them.

"I'm sorry." His tone holds confusion and hesitancy as his arms fall away from me. "I—I thought you were attracted to me."

"Well I have shitty taste in men, so *obviously* I'm attracted to you." My lips snap closed before I say something embarrassing. Snark overpowers my tumbling emotions.

Why am I so stupid? Someone cares about me and my instinct is to shove them far, far away.

"So ... you can come on my mouth, but you can't kiss me?"

Yes! Thankfully he understands completely. I knew he and I were alike. We're both a little damaged because of our pasts and thank the goddess he understands that.

His hand pushes slowly across his face, his jaw locking together before he finally leans into me and speaks in a low and rumbling tone. His silence is pushed aside as his frustration growls through him.

"How about I just never touch you again and neither of us will be confused about what part of me is good enough for you."

There's always this back and forth between us. Our emotions are too unsteady for us to ever be on the same page.

My lips part with a reply but giant white wings burst from his back and glinting scales cover his shoulders, turning the flesh right before my eyes at a rapid pace. He looks like an archangel. Beautiful and deadly. A man of solid strength, and anger, and wings as pure as snow. Stormy eyes glare back at me just before he fully changes, being swept away in a fume of magic. The beast that stands before me lowers his head and, for a moment, I think he'll offer me a ride like he did before.

Then his powerful wings thrust down, shoving harshly

at the wind as he takes flight. The breeze sweeps up my hair, twirling it messily across my face as I watch him soar away.

"Such a dramatic exit." I huff a sigh, pretending hard not to feel the sting of his words in my chest. On slow steps I pick up the glass bowl. Ash drifts along the top of the water as I stare down at Bobble. He blows me a few little bubbles, the only sign that he cares.

I look to Grim and the dog lowers his ears before making his way toward me. These two care about me. These two will always be here for me. Nothing could take these sweet creatures from me.

We were almost friends, Rime and me.

Thank the Goddess I avoided that.

"We need to lay low for a while until we can figure out what to do with her." Kain looks at me like I'm a broken thing he doesn't know how to fix.

No one asked him to fix me. If I had my money right now, I would be well on my way to a new and improved life.

An involuntary smile pulls at my lips as Agatha's frail hands skim against the smooth span of Chaos' chest. Her fingers push over his shoulders, feeling at the hard muscle there before veering down. Chaos tilts his head at me, but he lets the woman feel her fill.

I set Bobble's bowl on the counter, pushing back a

mound of old newspapers to make a little space for the fish. He wobbles in his little glass home as he looks out at the towering papers above him. Before he even starts to drift up, I push the slick scales of his back and send him right back down into the safety of his water.

"It's been a few decades since I've had young men in my life. Want to make sure I get a proper fit for you boys." Blindly, she feels along until her palms are pushing against Rime's body. He watches her closely, and I have to admit, I'm a little jealous she has an excuse for her blatant fondling. She moves on to the next one. Kain all but bites her hand like a dog as he glares down on the little old woman who's stroking down his abdomen. When her fingertips skim his hips, he jerks back from her. "Hmm, I guess that's enough to go on." With an arch of her slender fingers, and a turn of her wrist, clothes fall from the ceiling. Jeans, shirts and boots land in a heap of a pile on the old dusty floor.

"Why couldn't you do that?" Kain looks to me, and I am really proud of myself for not sticking my tongue out at his condescending tone. I'm honestly too exhausted from all the magic I've used today to fight with him. "You're this powerful mage, right?"

I don't tell him how tired I am from everything that's happened. I also don't mention how much my magic has been hidden way nearly all my life.

I'm not weak, not really. But I'm not as powerful as Aggie either.

My lips part but Agatha jumps in. She turns to him, her long silver hair twirling like a cape behind her.

"Magic progresses with age and studying, boy. Do not talk down on a young mage, for when she is an Elder, you will surely fear her."

"So, in fifty years, you'll be a force to be reckoned with?" Kain cocks his fucking fiery brow at me.

Agatha grew up in a society that embraced magic; that fed from it, and trained it, and empowered it. She's told me tales how she was the most loved woman in all of Minden once. And now she hides away from the very people who once cared so much for her.

My magic has been hidden away all my life. It's been hidden and saved up even more in the last five years since I've been running from my demons. Literally.

I can't find it in me to reply to him. My throat tightens as I realize I'm barely a mage at all most days. What a waste of power. This is how it was when I was a child, and this is how it is now that I'm an adult. I'm still hiding myself. Nothing has changed.

My feet skim against the flooring and, in just three quiet steps, I'm outside. I pull the door closed behind me and lower myself down against the cottage. Dry dirt pushes through my fingertips. A hum of a whine catches my attention, and Grim circles next to me before lying down and settling his massive head in my lap.

I stroke his warm fur slowly, letting the ash coat my palm as I delve my fingers into his thick hair.

A mess of thoughts circle my mind.

The men finally got what they came for; a mage. Now I've dragged them into my problems. I should leave. I should sneak out tonight and give them the easy way out. But I know that's not the easy way. I don't know why they owe Kreedence, but he'll never let them free until they do what they agreed to do.

So, we're all fucked.

Black boots stand at my side, and I don't look up at him as he pulls the door closed. Chaos' shoulder skims against mine as he lowers himself to sit next to me. Neither of us speaks and it's nice. I like the silence right now. I like the way the sky is a slate of white with a hue of pale orange emitting within it. Everything is beautiful on the surface right now. A beautiful evening, a beautiful man, and a beautiful woman.

It's what's beneath the surface that's ugly.

"I'm not like Rime or Kain." *That's for sure.* I keep my snarky comments to myself as Chaos continues, "I can't seem to take life serious enough, and it gets me into so much shit. The only reason we met you is because I picked a fight with Kreedence. He bet me he could win in a fistfight. I didn't ask what the winner would win."

"You didn't?" What an idiot.

"No, I was drunk at a pub a few cities over, and he said, 'you're not nearly as tough as you think you are.' Or something. Then he said, 'I bet I could beat you in a fist fight.'"

His hands clasp together, his arms settling against his bent knees as we look out at the washed-out skyline.

"What did you say?"

"Nothing. I fucking hit him." There's a hint of a smile against his lips, and my fingers leave Grim's fur, hesitantly touching Chaos' arm.

He is definitely an idiot. I can't believe he picked a fight against a demon.

And lost.

He's not one to back down, I suppose.

"I think you're stronger than you think. Maybe you're used to being told you're weak, but you're not weak." There's a sound of awe in his voice that warms my chest when he looks over at me. "I just, I wanted to tell you, it doesn't matter how strong or powerful you are." His head tilts, his gaze watching the way my fingers are skimming against his arm before he finally meets my eyes. "Everybody fucks up in life, Low."

My heart's thundering in my chest. It's a feeling of weak and uncontrollable emotions. He makes me feel like my endless screw ups aren't this massive weight I'm carrying around. That my power's strong even when it's hidden.

It's definitely improving. I guess. Years ago, I'd never be able to do everything I did today.

The warm feel of his hand against mine makes me lean into him. A faint growl from Grim causes me to pause for only a second before my head settles against Chaos' shoulder. It's nice. It's nice to have someone to comfort me. I'm surrounded by his strength and Grim's warmth, and everything feels completely perfect.

For one full minute.

"Cuddle time is over. We need to get moving," Rime's boots stomp down the weak boards of Aggie's porch.

"We're not leaving until dawn," I yell after him. I stand quickly and take a few steps toward him, but I refuse to chase him down. I stop after only a few steps, standing between the two men.

Really, I'm just stalling. I'm still not sure if I want to be tied to them, but we are in similar situations. It's just ... I've never had a companion, let alone three companions. I'm not good at having someone I care so much about.

It's terrifying.

"Let's go." His shoulders stiffen with every command he barks.

"I'm not going." My arms fold across my chest, and his attention pulls there to my breasts. I'm very aware of how thin my clothes are, but I've never put as much thought into my shirt as Rime is right now.

Rime quickly looks away, but Chaos' warm attention is still pinned to the outline of my breasts. I force myself not to look down to see what he sees.

"You have to go. This isn't up for discussion." Rime's words make my jaw clench.

I've spent the last five years with only myself and Grim to protect me. I don't need these men.

"Prove to me you two can take care of me better than Grim can and I'll go." My head tilts at him, daring the aggressive man when I know I've already pissed him off today.

"I think you and I both know how good I can take care of you." Chaos' low tone hums against my hair, and I have to shift away from him and that alluring sound or I'll relent and follow him wherever his sexy voice wants to take me.

"Prove it." I cock my head at him and a smile pulls at his lips.

"Prove it?" Chaos' eyes narrow on me; his mind is probably a spiral of dirty thoughts.

"If Rime were attacking me, how would you fight him off? Impress me." I already know Chaos isn't one to back down, and his next words make a warm feeling flood my body from how quickly he gives in to me.

"How would he be positioned? I need more details if you want me to protect your virtue and shit."

My lips part with a taunting reply against my lips, but then Rime is stalking toward me. His confidence isn't playful like Chaos'. There's no teasing undertone to his actions. He has a look of dangerous aggression with slow steps that make words slip away from me.

He passes me and the chilling look in his eyes shivers right through me. The cruel set of his mouth makes me wonder what he isn't saying. That's all I ever think when I consider his silence. Because he's always thinking but never speaking.

In silence, he pushes his chest against my back. My spine stiffens beneath his touch as his palms travel slowly down my ribs, teasing my skin with his light touch before gripping my hips hard. The memory of his mouth against my body is all I can think about as I shift against him. I force my arms over my chest, trying hard to prove he doesn't affect me.

Especially since just an hour ago, he promised to never touch me again. His head tilts toward mine just slightly, resting against me in a gentle way.

"So ... this would be an attack?" A smirk tilts Chaos' lips as he cocks a brow at Rime in a knowing way. It seems to amuse him to know his friend is attracted to me.

In less than a second, Rime jerks me hard against his chest, pushing the air from my lungs with his controlling touch. Strong arms wrap over mine, holding me in a captive but romantic position against him. Warm breath fans against my neck, and I have to put real effort into stifling the heavy exhale that falls from my lips. I'm insanely aware of how wet my panties are right now. My nerves are a bundle of tight energy within my core, and all I can think about is the bulge that's pressing hard against my lower back.

Chaos takes a stalking step closer. Closer and closer, he advances like a calculating beast ready to strike. His fists rise, and without holding back, he aims for Rime's face that's so close to mine. My breath catches as Rime pulls me to the left. I stagger but his swift movement avoids Chaos' blow.

My lungs heave against the tight hold Rime has on me. To distract him, to prove he's not as capable as he should be, I roll my hips, letting my ass shift nicely against his dick.

He groans but keeps his hold on me, and it only makes me want to shift harder; to hear him really lose that control he always clings to.

Until I realize I've distracted him too much.

A half smile is against Chaos' lips as his fist lands hard against Rime's jaw, and even I flinch away from the sound of the thudding impact.

Once more, Chaos comes closer, not giving Rime even a second to process the pain. The two men are fully fighting now, letting me be the common ground between them. Rime waits until Chaos is near enough, his fist raised for another blow, before Rime grips his friend's shirt and pulls hard. Chaos' body is warm against mine, but he's only there for a second. Rime slams his head against Chaos'. The impact makes the two men stagger back from one another. My fingers dig into Rime's arm as we stumble together, but he never releases me.

Chaos groans but a smile tilts his lips.

He's so strong, he'll never let this end without real harm coming to both of them. I remember the way they tumbled around my house, play fighting as small dragons, and I can't help but wonder if this is a normal thing for them as men as well.

The two men are stalking right back toward one another, letting me stumble along with them. I'm just about to speak when Rime does something I couldn't have anticipated even if I was a fucking mind reader.

He grips the back of Chaos neck, and I flinch away when I fear their heads will slam together again.

But it never happens.

Rime slams his lips against Chaos', forcing the affection in a way that doesn't appear affectionate at all. Tension is held in their bodies for a moment. Every muscle in Rime's arm is lined with strength, and I'm pressed between their hard bodies, staring up in awe as Chaos' lips tilt into another slow smile. A hum of laughter shakes through him just before his lips part and he meets Rime's tongue slowly with a gentle caress. Rime's fingers tense slightly against Chao's neck as they take their time.

My breath is heavy as it falls hard over my lips. I've never put so much thought and attention on Rime's cruel mouth. Confusion swirls through me when Rime's grip on me changes. His palm pushes low down my abdomen, burning across my skin as his fingers halt just beneath the elastic of my skirt. My fingers trail up Chaos' chest, and his big hands lock onto my waist pulling me even closer to him as his head tilts to kiss Rime harder. A sound that's similar to a moan shakes from my lungs as my ass grinds against Rime's cock.

All the confusion I felt moments ago is quickly forgotten as I let their fingers explore my body. The kiss deepens, their jaws working in the sexiest way I've ever seen. And I'm at the center of their pleasure. Rime's gentle touch pushes lower, just above where I want him most, and he groans against Chaos' lips.

He shoves back from us, forcefully pushing away from Chaos as well as myself. The heat of his touch is replaced with the cool wind as I stand confused once again.

It was the sexiest thing I've ever seen, and it ended before it even began.

I look from one man to the other. Chaos holds a smoldering smile in his features while Rime still looks ... completely pissed off.

"Did that impress you?" Rime's words make a scowl pull at my lips.

This is why I'll never allow a man to kiss me ever again. Life and love, it's all just a mess.

"Do you guys ... always do that?" It's a stupid question, but I can't seem to stop it from coming out of my mouth.

"No. I've never kissed Chaos before."

"But you've thought about it, right?" Chaos' smile is wide and taunting as his attention skims over every inch of Rime's body.

Rime doesn't look at his friend.

"I just wanted to prove that sometimes a kiss doesn't mean anything."

The door bangs shut behind us, but I don't turn to see who's watching.

"I know." My voice shakes and I swallow hard against the pathetic feel of my emotions. I'm just so astounded that he's completely misunderstood me. "Sometimes it means too much to one person, and it means absolutely nothing to the other. And, *sometimes*, it ruins everything. Thanks for reminding me of that."

His features soften slightly. The hard angles of his jaw no longer tic with fury, and his glaring eyes hold the smallest hint of pity there.

I think I like it better when he's irrationally angry. At least, then I know how to speak to him. Right now, I don't know what to even say.

So, I say nothing.

An awkward beat passes and I consider leaving them here, turning away and hiding inside from their blunt explanations.

But Chaos beats me to it.

In an inky swirl of acidic tinged magic, he changes form. Dark scales crawl across the flesh of his forearms until the dragon within him consumes him entirely. The playful dragon lunges for Rime and the man steps back with caution but, in a matter of seconds, he shifts to defend himself against his friend.

Their sharp teeth snap at one another, nearly nicking each other's neck but just nipping at the rough scales as they run around the small yard. It seems more intimate now than it did the last time they played like this. Until Rime bucks his head up, aiming his sharp horns for Chaos' chest. The dragon barely rolls away in time to protect himself, his body almost colliding with Grim's. The hellhound gives a low rumbling sound of disapproval before stalking off to a more secluded part of Agatha's garden.

For several moments, I just watch the two dragons play and fight one another in a mass of claws and teeth and groaning growls. The amount of time I consider how Rime's teeth linger on Chaos' throat starts to become an overanalyzed thought within my mind.

Rime is shit at showing his emotions. But this feels ... affectionate in a way. It's as natural as breathing for these two.

"They've always been better at fighting one another than talking." Kain doesn't look to me as he comes to my side, keeping his gaze fixed on his friends who just wiped out the old wooden awning that covered over Agatha's well. The wood crumbles beneath their massive paws before they carry on to the next space to destroy.

"They're good at fighting." My head tilts as Chaos swoops up high to dodge his friend's roaring attack. Dark wings push hard, swirling the dirt around me as he lifts himself higher and higher.

"They're so much better at fighting than anything else." A pause drifts between his words for a moment. "They don't have much experience with anything else, I guess. Neither of them knows the pain and reality of love. That excited fear that pounds through your heart isn't even a thought inside their heads." He isn't angry with me like he was earlier. There's a gentleness to his words. I can't help but wonder if he heard my emotional outburst.

My lips part, and I realize Kain and I might have more in common than he's letting on. The four of us are used to being defensive, but none of us are very good at simply talking about our feelings. I might have had a normal life at one time, but it's been long forgotten.

Friendship, and just normal conversation, isn't my strong suit.

Not at all.

No matter how hard I try.

As insufferable as these assholes may be, I'm just like them.

EIGHTEEN

FLAWS AND FUCK UPS

An orange hue of warm sunlight hits my golden skin as I wait for it to fade away into dusk. Rime sits next to me on the small steps, shirtless and in a pair of jeans that fit a little too snugly, watching Chaos' dragon form doze in the dirt. There's a silence to the man just like there always is, but he seems to be really staring at the dragon. Considering him in a way; making me wish I could understand all the things Rime never says.

Chaos' dragon is enormous. From the tip of his snout all the way down to the curve of his tail, he's larger than Aggie's cottage. His face is bigger than my body. He could literally swallow me in one bite like a midday snack.

Why do I find myself wishing I could be his snack ...

"You really should learn some defensive moves for yourself." Kain's statement pulls at my attention until I peer up at him. He leans against the door behind me, his pale eyes held on the sunset as the lighting casts across his smooth skin, warming it just slightly.

"What makes you think I don't already know defensive moves?" My tone is confident even though I only know how to sucker punch someone, and that's if they're extremely close and directly in front of me.

For the most part, I just depend on my magic. Too bad I hide it away from the world.

"You won't always have beasts to protect you."

A low growl emits from somewhere beneath the bushes, and it seems that Grim would care to disagree with the shifter.

"You think you're going to train me to be an expert fighter in a few hours?"

His thigh pushes against my shoulders and he passes me, looking back at me as he stalks into the middle of the dusty road.

"I could teach you a thing or two." There's almost humor in his words. It's a flirting, tingling tone really.

It's ... weird.

Rime's gaze shifts to me, but he keeps his heavy silence even as I stand. The ground is cool beneath my feet, and I take my time meeting him in the middle of the worn roadway.

The slow drag of his attention across my body makes me shift on my feet. I don't know what's changed between us. Since this morning, since my small breakdown, he seems to notice me now.

Almost too much.

"Ready?" His taunting tone makes my nerves prickle anxiously, and it's hard for me to keep my carelessness as I raise my palms from my sides in a casual shrug.

He's shit at protecting his left side.

My eyes widen. Chaos' voice whispers through my mind. It distracts me and confuses me, but when I look to him, he seems to still be napping. His tail sweeps across the ground back and forth in a slow motion as if he's not even aware of it at all.

Did I really just hear him in my thoughts?

I've studied all creatures, every beautiful one of them, but the information on rare beasts like dragons is limited. Our world doesn't have the beautiful deadly creatures roaming the land like it once did. None of my books ever mentioned a telepathic trait between them and humans, and these men haven't shown me anything like that the entire time they've been here.

Perhaps ... I imagined it. Or perhaps dragon shifters are more different than I realized. I haven't been around them long enough to form any kind of bond like Chaos mentioned.

Have I?

Kain takes slow, tormenting steps that seem to draw out my anticipation of what he's about to do. His hand raises in a defensive stance and, just like Chaos said, it's his right hand.

Now's my window.

Right now.

My fingers dig into my palm and the knuckles of my

hand sting against his jaw. Maybe it was a sucker punch, maybe it was expert timing. Maybe it was a little of both. Either way, triumph soars through me.

This is what winning feels like.

"Oh, shit," Rime says with a hint of laughter kissing his tone.

"What the fuck, Arlow?" Kain's brows pull low as his palm pushes across his face, his gaze glaring down on me hard.

"I—I thought you said you were ready." The excitement and accomplishing feeling of making the first move sizzles right out of me.

"Do you know what defense means? I wasn't going to attack you. I was going to show you how to defend yourself. Fuck."

Laughter continues to hum from the man behind me, and I throw a quick look at Chaos to find his large gleaming eyes watching the two of us intently. A sort of amused look is in his two-toned gaze.

Asshole.

"Don't use your magic either." He takes another step toward me, but he halts the moment I speak.

"I can't."

"You can't?" His head dips, his attention shifting over my features as I look at every single detail of the dark forest behind him to avoid his curious gaze.

I shouldn't have told him that. It's stupid to tell them how much of myself I hide away from the world.

I guess I'm all in now. It's terrifying to know I'll actually depend on them in the future. It's terrifying that I trust them right now.

This whole time they were looking for a mage. Well, now they have her. Now they know she's not nearly as impressive and marveling as they were told.

"I've never had much training to be a mage. With the laws changing, with mages becoming hunted, my parents hid my magic. I was ... a burden on them. They hid me away most of my life. So much so that I hadn't even used my magic until I was an adult and even now I hide it. I save it in case I have a run in with Kreedence. I won't waste it on training, Kain."

I hate that this special thing about me makes me a danger to myself. To my family. To society even.

"You disappeared pretty well on me," Rime says in an even but pointed tone.

"I'm exceptionally good at hiding. At disappearing. I've had a lifetime of experience in that department. But using it like that tires me. It's not as easy as it should be. It's ... pathetic really."

Moments pass as the three of them stare at me in a heavy and pressing silence.

"Rime can't tell directions when he's in his dragon form. Can't tell north from south if it's high noon." Kain's honest but random statement throws me off guard.

"Fuck you, my eyes can't pick up on the sunlight and shit." Rime's defensive tone makes Kain smile.

"Chaos is a full adult dragon and still can't grow his horns."

A grumbling growl comes from the dark dragon before he rolls away slowly, giving us the span of his long tail as he chooses to look to the woods instead of us.

Poor baby always being reminded of his flaws.

A smile pulls at my lips, but I still don't know where he's going with this.

"I hate people. I'm not good at trusting them. Especially women. I've felt the start of a mating bond once and it … she fucked me over." His attention is on the ground between us as he says it, far, far away from my curious gaze.

Huh. He's just like me.

A strange sort of anger fumes through me at whoever the woman was who hurt him.

He shifts his weight, pulling his attention from the dirt to meet my gaze.

"My point is we're all fucked up, Arlow. But those flaws don't get to decide who we are. You're powerful. I know it. I've seen it." A pause drifts between his words. "I feel it." Energy swirls through my chest at the sound of his appraisal. In just two short steps, he's close enough to touch. So close that his fingers drift across the back of my knuckles, not holding my hand but just lightly skimming against my skin. Making me crazy with the fluttering feeling within my stomach. "Let me help you."

The sincerity of his voice sinks right into me. It's all I feel strumming through my veins.

He really thinks he could help me?

The warm sound of his voice makes me realize I trust them all too much.

Because I want nothing more in the world than for him to help me.

Even if I know it's a terrible idea for two emotionally broken people.

NINETEEN

PERSONAL SPACE

"You know you're wasting them, right?" Aggie's voice is conspiratorial sound.

With a wave of her hand, she provides me with a new pair of clothes almost identical to the swaying skirt and shirt I always wear. Her bedroom is a darker space, but just as cluttered as her living room. Stacks of old newspapers stand taller than me in the corner, and I eye it with a worried look as it teeters but doesn't fall.

"I just think if there are three very muscular men in your life, you should take advantage of your good fortune. The Goddess has clearly blessed you for a good deed."

A good deed. Not likely, Aggie.

"Have you even felt number three's arms? Good Goddess, what is he lifting with those arms? Mmm imagine what he's lifting, Low. Imagine it."

My eyes close slowly as I realize she's numbered them based off of who she felt up during her line up.

Number three; I do a quick recap. Number three is Kain.

"Oh, the things I would do to those men if my bad hip was twenty years younger. I should have taken better care of that damn hip."

A smile pulls at my lips.

"I'm going to take a shower." She needs a cold shower too, I think, but I'm not going to mention it.

As I step past her, her thin hand slips around mine. It's a light touch, a gentle touch, and I think it's the first time we've ever touched actually.

"Really though. I—I think they want to help you. Let them help you, Low." She hesitates for only a moment, perhaps testing me to see if I'll agree. When I don't, she continues. "Not all men are bad. I promise; some are so loyal, so loving, so irreplaceable."

Her odd words linger in the silence.

Sometimes, I think Aggie is wise.

And, sometimes, I think she's shut herself away here for so long she's forgotten what the real world is like.

I envy her for that.

The real world is shit. I'll let her live in that pleasant fairytale for the rest of her life.

"I'm sorry for bringing you into this." My whispered words make her silver brows pull together.

A beat passes before she releases my hand and walks past me.

"We're a family." She pauses for a moment, letting her words warm my chest. "I knew you'd take good care of those dragon shifters." My lips part as I try to process her words, my thoughts going all the way back to the first night that she buried them right in front of me. "You're sweeter than you act, Low." She squeezes my hand lightly before trailing on a hobbling step to the door. "But you're a stubborn woman," she mumbles before she leaves.

I trail away from her cramped bedroom and into the only bathroom in the little cottage. The small room is filled with old newspapers along the wash sink. Orange, fading sunshine casts across the space, and I toss my clothes in the only empty spot along the floor, letting my skirt and shirt take space among the dusty books.

At some point in Agatha's long life, she must not have been blind. She must have loved these things she surrounds herself with even if she can no longer appreciate them. I don't have anything sentimental in my life. I left my parents years ago, and I haven't really settled anywhere since. There are no brothers or sisters to share fond memories with. I've never stayed in one place long enough to collect friends.

There is only me.

And, most of the time, that's how I like it. At least, that's what I thought.

There's a metal plate high on the rock tile wall, and I push it aside to release a gushing flow of water. It falls from the hole in the wall with a steady outpour that hits my shoulders when I step into the chilling water. A gasp leaves my throat but, in just a moment, I become used to the feel of it and the tension leaves my body in an instant. The gentle pressure falls across my skin, drenching my hair as I tip my face up and inhale the fresh scent.

It's perfectly relaxing.

It's so relaxing I start to become comfortable with the idea of having a friendship with these men. They care about me. It isn't the most blatant appearance of kindness, but I can see it.

I can feel it.

The sound of the door clicking closed has the tension snapping right back into place. I peer past the damp stone wall and meet shining emerald eyes. They trail down the length of my bare skin, making me wish there was a dividing wall of some kind separating the bathing area from the rest of the room.

I know Aggie lives alone, and the poor woman is blind for Goddess' sake, but a little bit of coverage would be appreciated right now.

"What you said outside, about kissing being cut off emotionally, I don't agree." Kain's words don't hold his normal, harsh tone. It's just a statement. He's always the one with a plan. Always plotting.

It makes me watch him a little more carefully.

The thudding of his boots against the old floorboards holds my attention. He doesn't hesitate as he steps right in. The water beats down against his clothes. It soaks through his white shirt, sticking deliciously to every line of his hard body. Heat drifts between us, but the slickness of the water streaming over my skin makes my thighs shift.

My arms fold defensively across my chest, below the underside of my breasts, amplifying the curves, but I don't hide them. I pretend I'm not at all affected by his presence. His gaze follows the beading water that's slipping down my skin and across my nipples.

I try to ignore the way his attention makes energy pool right to the center of my sex.

"Do you mind? My water's getting colder, and I don't remember giving you an invitation." My tone is clipped, but I'm not able to contain the breathy sound following my words.

"I'll be sure not to waste your time then." His rumbling words are low and smooth.

He takes a single, dominant step closer to me. I lean slightly back from him. My feet won't move, but my body still pretends not to want him.

He closes the minimal space between us. The drenched t-shirt is rough against my nipples, and I'm suddenly arching into him for a whole new reason. My arms remain folded, my nails sinking tightly into my palms. A smirk tilts his lips as his fingers slip through the base of my hair. He tips my head roughly back for him, and I watch his every move with firmly held lips. My jaw is angled high, his grip tightening in my hair. My gaze slips for only an instant to his beautiful mouth.

"You wouldn't dare." I threaten his intent, and I

realize it's the wrong thing to do to a man who never listens to a thing I say.

"Mmm, yes I fucking would," he says on a whisper. "You want me to kiss you? To make you feel like you matter to me?"

The warmth of his breath fans against my lips, and I can't seem to find a response in my mind. There's something in Kain that's different. It's the way he watches me. The way he watches everyone really. The skeptical cautiousness in him matches everything about me.

We're the same.

That thought alone makes up my mind. Slowly I nod to him, keeping my gaze locked with his.

He searches my eyes. Every second that passes strikes through my body with buzzing energy that I feel in the most sensitive places.

His head dips lower. His lips press firmly against mine, but he isn't forceful. It's a chaste kiss.

It's ... surprisingly perfect.

It's everything I didn't know I craved. His closeness, his body against mine, his gentleness; it's all more perfect than I ever could have imagined.

No one's touched me like this in so long. It feels more intimate than anything else. It makes me ache for more. I feel his kiss building within my chest, twirling through my stomach and pulsing between my thighs.

Water rains down on us, attempting to cool the heat between our bodies. The slick feel of his big palm sliding low against my back wakes me up inside as our hips align, his jeans against my flesh. My fingers fist in the hem of his shirt, and I relax beneath his touch. I part my lips, wanting more, wanting to feel every inch of him. Just lightly, his tongue flicks along mine, almost making me moan from the small movement.

And then he pulls away.

A smile clings to his mouth as his tongue rolls slowly across his bottom lip. Water clings to the tips of his fiery hair, threatening to fall right into his deep green eyes.

He looks pleased with himself.

The arrogant dragon taint.

With another long and appreciative look down my body, his hands slip away from me. He moves slowly back, putting cold air between us, smiling that shit-eating smile the whole time. My arms cross once more, and he carefully steps away. Water clings to his steps, leaving puddles in his wake.

"You're making everything wet."

I curse myself the moment I say it.

"No need to scream about your wetness, Arlow." He walks backward, and he holds my gaze as the serious look settles back into his eyes. "I just wanted you to know that it didn't feel like nothing to me." He pauses just long enough for his rumbling tone to sink into me. "I wanted you to feel that."

His words twist warmth all through me, and the feeling smothers out the annoyance in me until all I feel is that building emotion of happiness. My head meets the wall, letting the chilly water beat against the back of my neck.

Fuck, I let him kiss me.

And I liked it.

Goddess, why did I like it?

TWENTY

HER DEMONS

Agatha set out blankets patched from miscellaneous fabric patterns. The frayed edges of the quilts show their age, but they're soft and comforting. Chaos made a pallet on the floor and has settled in there. Rime and Kain talk quietly near the window. Rime's pale eyes never stop sweeping over the darkness even as he speaks.

I meet those shining, mossy colored eyes and a small smile pulls at the corner of Kain's mouth, just the slightest tilting of his lips before he looks away, pushing that serious appearance right back into place. He's constantly so damn somber.

But he showed me a different sort of seriousness tonight.

The swirling feeling in my chest is pushed away, and I'm so distracted I don't even realize I'm settling in next to Chaos before the damage is already done. I sit there an inch from him as he lies on his back. He's always so quick to settle in against me, but it feels odd for me to do it to him.

"Stop thinking so much." He lifts his arm to me, offering me the inviting space at his side.

With stiff movements, I lower myself. My head rests awkwardly high on his chest, not anywhere near his arm, and I lie there gracelessly like a dog searching for affection from her master.

This is ridiculous.

I shift, pushing to turn away from him to just lie on the hard floor. At the last second, his arm wraps around my stomach, pulling me against his chest in a warm and comforting way. My body reacts to him, melding perfectly with his as my head rests against his bicep.

"Was that so hard?" he whispers against my hair, his head leaning against mine.

"Yes."

He breathes out a smile that I feel within myself even. The simplicity of the moment starts to slip away as I remember how his voice skimmed through my thoughts.

"How was I able to hear your thoughts, Chaos?"

The way his body stiffens against mine, his arm tensing beneath my touch, makes my nerves prickle all through me. He's keeping something from me.

"Chaos?" I whisper his name, but I never turn to look at him.

"I—" His tone hums against my body. "Sometimes when shifters fuck ..." Well this is an interesting start to a story. "Sometimes the dragon side of them tries to create a bond. Dragons are loyal by nature."

A bond. That sounds entirely too intimate.

"A bond? Like ... friendship?"

A beat passes and his palm feels heavier against my stomach.

"No, like ... a mating bond."

My eyes widen as those words settle right into my mind. I turn abruptly until my gaze is glaring up into his beautiful eyes.

"You created a fucking mating bond between us, and you didn't think to tell me?" The sound of my harsh whisper scrapes through the room.

His palm still holds me against him as he slowly seems to think about the best way to say whatever it is that's in his head.

"Not exactly, no. It's not a full-on bond. It's just a primitive reaction. We fucked. My dragon form wants that connection. It physically wants a mate. That doesn't mean my emotions allow it, Low." There's sincerity in his eyes, and I can tell he's really trying not to worry me.

"Would your dragon have done it with anyone you slept with?" I don't know why I ask him that. Why do I want his response so badly?

"What? No. It's hard to explain. Compatibility, attraction, and something completely out of my control makes a mating bond click into place." His gaze searches mine, looking for something there before he speaks in a rumbling whisper. "My dragon wants a mate and it ... it likes the way I like you if that makes sense."

His dragon likes the way he likes me. A flutter of emotions storms through me at his awkwardly romantic words.

His dragon form primitively wants a mate; I understand that. It's natural, I suppose, to want that connection. It's natural for humans, and it's natural for a lot of creatures.

"For you was it just fucking?" I don't know why my voice just quivered as I said that.

I clear my throat before meeting his gaze once again.

"I wouldn't say it was just fucking. I—I like you. We're friends. Aren't we?"

I consider his words as if his dragon form might sneakily lure me into some sort of mating contract without me realizing it. Slowly, I nod to him.

My shoulders relax as I stiffly lie back down, trying hard to find the comfort his body gave me just moments ago.

"We're friends." His lips skim against my neck, his beard scraping sensually against my skin. "We're friends who fuck. Friends who fuck really, really good." His tongue meets my flesh before his teeth rake gently along my throat, sending a tingling feeling right through my core. I have to bite back the heavy breath against my lips.

"Good night, K," I say very pointedly.

I don't know why he thinks now is the time to confuse his dragon side even further. No, we won't be confusing the creature any more with sex. A bond is the very last thing I need in my life.

He hums a quiet laugh against my neck before settling down behind me, holding me to his chest in an embrace of calming sensations. The gentle way he holds me is like nothing I've ever felt. I was in love once, and yet I've never experienced contentment and simple happiness like this.

Everything feels right in the world.

Kain glances back at me. It's a quick look from beneath his lashes as if he's checking on me every few moments.

Rime still won't acknowledge me. He's choosing to surveil the darkness instead. I can't help but stare at him, watching his every careful move. Then he looks at me, his pale eyes locking with mine, sinking me with a single look. There's no anger in him, just an empty stare like his mind isn't turning at all as he watches me. It's like there's nothing else he's thinking of. Just me. Kain's words catch against his lips as he turns to find his friend focused entirely on me.

The tingling feeling of their attention makes my eyes close, forcing the weight of their gazes away from me. A quiet breath leaves my lungs.

In a weird way, for the first time in years, I feel like I'm right where I should be. I'm not running—not yet—and I'm not worried.

Everything feels perfect. What are the odds Chaos would piss off the same demon I pissed off? That one terrible choice in his life brought the four of us together.

I'm fairly sure this is what fate must feel like.

In my dreams he visits me again, comforting me and tormenting me with his memory.

His strong body melds against mine and all I can think about is the concern that's hidden in his fiery eyes this time. There isn't that look of love or desire. Not this time. This time there's only a deep appearance of worry lining his sharp features.

Confusion drifts through my mind. Small details of the dream changes from time to time but one thing always stays the same.

That damn life destroying, soul consuming, terribly beautiful kiss.

Despite the peculiar look in his eyes, my heart hammers hard, begging to be near him. I lean into him. My gaze holds his as out lips nearly touch.

But then he speaks.

"Arrie, wake up." The whispered words feel warm against my skin.

My mouth parts, my brows pulling low as I process what he just said.

"Wake up now, love."

"What?" My fingers tighten into his soft shirt. Heat radiates from him and into me.

"Wake up *right* now."

I feel him. I feel him all around me, more than I have in five straight years.

"Sinister ..." Confusion tinges my tone and a trickle of fear sinks through me. It's something I can't explain. It's the sensation of prickling anxiety and just knowing that something bad is about to happen. It's a feeling of knowing, despite not knowing.

That feeling only intensifies when he speaks again.

"Arrie, he's coming."

My eyes flash open. A heaving breath shutters in my lungs. The slamming sound of my heartbeat drills through my ears.

And fiery red eyes look down on me.

Grim's big paws are against my shoulders, his weight held above me as he lets out a low, whimpering whine that crawls through the room. The heat of his body suffocates me despite the front door that's swinging open in the wind. The breeze chills the room but his nearness stifles the feel of the cold night air.

His soft fur is fisted in my fingers just as Sinister's shirt was. Chaos' hand is low against my stomach. Kain's chest is solid against my arm as he holds me against him.

Flat on my back I look up at the hellhound and those words claw through my mind on repeat.

He's coming. He's coming. He's coming.

The smoke wafting off of the beast's fur starts to intensify, burning brighter in the pale moonlight until it fogs the room entirely.

"Grim, are you okay, boy?" I push my fingers through his thick black fur but he only cries more. The sound carries on and the fear within me shifts to worry as the dog's eyes close with pain but I don't understand why.

Boots sound heavily against the floor but all I can focus on is the flinching agony in his features.

"He started yelping a few minutes ago. I opened the door and he ran right to you," Rime whispers.

My attention shifts to him for only a moment before stroking my palm back and forth along Grim's ears.

"It's okay. It's okay." A tightness constricts in my chest because I have no idea if it's really okay.

It certainly doesn't look okay.

More smoke clouds the room and I stifle a cough but my shoulders shake enough to jostle the two men at my sides. I sense it the moment they wake. I don't know when I became so aware of them. The simple change of their breathing is enough for me to know. It's the subtlest change of their bodies but I'm immensely aware of it. Chaos' fingers tense against my skin and Kain shifts until he's nearly sitting up.

"Are you okay?" Chaos looks from me to the hellhound above me.

I don't speak as I stare up at him, his fur heats to an unbearable feeling and that cry of his intensifies like a siren calling out a warning in the night. Inch by inch his fuming fur slips away into the smoke that surrounds us. It disappears into thin air. The beautiful beast that I love shifts right before my eyes.

It's replaced with a man I also once loved so. Damn. Much.

His body tenses beneath my touch as if pain is wrecking through him. My hands are still held on either side of his jaw, lightly touching his inky hair as he holds himself above me. The twisting tattoos along his bare arms tremble as his jaw clenches to repress the groan rumbling through his chest. His eyelids flinch harder together. He suppresses every single sound of his pain.

I've never seen him so weak in his entire life.

He looks like a man an inch from death.

And I have no idea if he is or not. Because I'm too astounded to even think clearly.

"He's coming." Shaking words rasp from his lips but I barely have time to hear him.

Big hands and violent strength tear him away from me. All at once the room erupts from anxious quietness into pandemonium. Rime grips his shoulders and slams the demon hard against the floor. The boards shake beneath us from the impact. Stacks of books come tumbling down around them in the white haze. Chaos and Kain leap onto him. The three of them hold him down. Their fists flex with intent.

But there's no struggle in the man pinned beneath them.

"Who the fuck are you?" Chaos growls.

Aggression charges the room. It's electric and growing. All I can do is watch them. I can't seem to move. I can't seem to think.

I can barely speak in the most breathlessly quiet voice.

"He's Sinister." The words sound hollow against my lips. Empty. Uncertain.

Iron hinges screech into the night. My attention rises to the darkness beyond the open door. An unnatural feeling makes the fine hair along my arms stand on end.

Magic burns against my fingertips. The stored magic within me is ready even if I'm not.

The three dragon shifters halt their aggression the moment I speak. Maybe it's my tone, maybe it's the shock that's shadowing my features.

Or maybe—just maybe—it's that sensation of knowing that something bad is about to happen.

Because what he once took from me he's now given back.

And that can only mean one thing ...

Kreedence is here.

The End.

AUTHOR'S NOTE

Thank you for reading Taming! Arlow and her darling little dragon taints have been consuming my thoughts for over six months now. I'm happy to say book two is finished because I can't stop writing about Arlow's endless antics and mysterious world. Book two, Claiming, is now available! Turn the page for a sneak peek at Claiming!

Order Claiming today!

KREEDENCE

I feel him long before I ever see him. He's in the nerves that claw through my body, he's in the rapid stumbling of my heart, he's in every shaking breath I take.

But especially, he's in the magic that snaps through my fingertips. With a burst of white light, the power rips from my palm. Through the quiet living room of Agatha's small cottage, out the open door, and into the dark night my magic soars. It seeks out a target with intent.

The three dragon shifters in the middle of the room still hover over Sinister. The demon looks more dead than alive, but that doesn't seem to deter the brooding shifters from pinning him to the floor. Silence stretches on as my fingers fist into the thin blanket covering me. The old floorboards beneath me were such a comfort when I slept, but sleep is the furthest thing in my mind now.

He's here. I feel it.

The bright light twirls, quickening its pace as if it's

about to reach a finish line. Magic bursts on impact with a flash of crimson as it strikes its target. That color bleeds light on the man lurking at the forest's edge.

Familiar red eyes eat up my features. The gentle breeze catches the tips of his inky hair. His head tilts with a smile slicing across his knowing lips. There's an acquainted look in his sharp features. The man looks at me like he knows everything about me.

Like he made me.

In a way, he has

I'm not that helpless little girl any more. I'm done running from him. I'm not afraid of Kreedence.

Not anymore.

The moment I see him, I stand. But I guess I'll never be as fast as a changing shifter.

The embers of light fade out softly and in an instant dark scales rip over Chaos' arms. He's barely out the door when wings burst from his back. He changes from the sweet man I've come to know into a storming, roaring beast.

The sound of the dragon's aggression tears through the night. I feel the rumbling of his anger in the shaking floorboards beneath my feet, the dress against my calves, the strands of my hair. In this moment, rage is a living, breathing thing.

I know Chaos is an unpredictable creature. There are too many emotions tearing through that man. And I see that clearly as his claws rip up the dirt and anger fumes from his snout.

A molten glow of orange and yellow drips from his lips, leaving a trail in the dirt. It sparks my interest even as the pretty colors start to burn into the earth.

It ... acid.

The light of it along the ground highlights the dragon's every move. Strong muscles flex with each step, inky scales glisten, power coils through every inch of the beast.

Rime stands, keeping his gaze locked on his friend as he takes quiet steps back. It takes me a moment to realize he's standing purposely in front of me, shielding me from the open door and whatever lurks beyond it. Kain remains kneeling on the floor. He keeps his big palm against Sinister's shoulder, as if the demon might somehow harm us in his unconscious state.

And Chaos is alone out there. Suddenly I am afraid. Fear trickles in and I shove past Rime to run after the reckless dragon. Jarring steps slow my pace as I stumble against the deep claw marks etching the ground. Tingling magic burns my fingertips as I fire shots into the dark forest in the distance. Magic brightens the world in streaming streaks of pure white. It teases the shadows. It warms the night. It reveals the demon waiting with patience for the beast ahead of me.

Color spews from Chaos' roaring mouth. Acid showers over the darkness. It lights up the surroundings like rain kissing the ground. It burns through nature itself. Leaves sizzle into nothingness. Tree bark cuts away inch by inch before the trees topple over onto one another. Acid stings the air and I can do nothing but breathe it in.

It's everywhere.

And yet, it missed its target.

White smoke wafts up. It burns a transparent memory of where Kreedence was just standing. My fingers tense against my palms with waiting magic as I stare wide eyed at the eerie emptiness of the night.

Warm breath and taunting words crawl down my spine.

"You didn't think you'd be rid of me so easily, did you?"

Order Claiming today!

If you want more Taming updates, giveaways, and special deleted dragon scenes sign up for my newsletter or join my Facebook Group!

A.K. Koonce Newsletter
A.K. Koonce Facebook Group

ALSO BY A.K. KOONCE

The Mortals and Mystics Series

Fate of the Hybrid, Prequel

When Fate Aligns, Book one

When Fate Unravels, Book two

When Fate Prevails, Book three

Resurrection Island, Stand Alone Book

Resurrection Island

The Royal Harem Series

The Hundred Year Curse

The Curse of the Sea

The Legend of the Cursed Princess

The Hopeless Series

Hopeless Magic

Hopeless Kingdom

Hopeless Realm

Hopeless Sacrifice

The Harem of Misery Series

Pandora's Pain

The Severed Souls Series

Darkness Rising

Darkness Consuming

Darkness Colliding

The Huntress Series

An Assassin's Death

An Assassin's Deception

ABOUT A.K. KOONCE

A.K. Koonce is a USA Today bestselling author. She's mom by day and a fantasy and paranormal romance writer by night. She keeps her fantastical stories in her mind on an endless loop while she tries her best to focus on her actual life and not that of the spectacular, but demanding, fictional characters who always fill her thoughts.

Made in the USA
Columbia, SC
02 September 2019